# Tangled up In You

**Bon Chance Boonies, Volume 1**

A. L. Vincent

Published by Bienvenue Press, 2021.

*For Cowboy*

You have always been one of the great loves of my life.
You taught me to never give up. Because of you, I
learned to always get back up and try again. I told you
the first book would be for you.

And for all the soldiers whose battles didn't end when
they came home.

*Semper Fi*

# Author's Note

It's been ten years since I first introduced the world of Bon Chance, and I still can't quite believe it.

When I first wrote *Tangled Up in You*, I had no idea how deeply this small-town world would resonate. What began as a love letter to second chances, porch swings, and slow-burning romance has grown into something much bigger. A three-book series with more on the way, a community, and a place readers have returned to again and again. For that, I'm endlessly grateful.

This updated edition is a little more polished, but at its heart, it's the same story of love, healing, and homecoming. If you've been with the Boonies from the beginning...thank you. Your support has meant more than I can ever say. And if you're just now discovering this world, welcome. I hope you feel right at home here.

Here's to the next chapter! And all the messy, beautiful, tangled up moments along the way.

Bon Chance and Happy Reading!

A.L. Vincent

# Acknowledgements

This book wouldn't have been possible without two people. Thank you Steve, for showing me that contest entry so many years ago, for your feedback, and for reading the manuscript a hundred times. Connie, you are such an inspiration to me. Thank you also, for reading my book multiple times and for all that you do!

Also, thanks goes to Denise for all of your support and for taking an awesome photo for my book cover.

Val, Ju, and Danyella, thanks for the Beta reads and the suggestions!

Thanks to everyone who offered me a story idea, or a word of encouragement on Facebook.

Curt Guillory, thanks for the feedback and help for the cook off scene.

And last but not least, thanks goes to all of the wonderful teachers I had along the way that encouraged my love for writing. Ms. Riggs, Ms. Drummonds, and Toby (I stopped calling you Dr. Daspit a long time ago!), you guys rock!

# Chapter One

"Run away to the Gulf Coast!" the billboard urged Emily Breaux as she rolled to a stop at the busy Lafayette intersection. She had just finished the morning shift at the diner, where she worked as a waitress and fill-in cook. The noon traffic was as heavy as her mood.

"I wish," she sighed. Growing up on the Gulf Coast, it would be more like running home. Brushing away tears, she glanced at the notice in the passenger seat. The rent was going up. She was already taking double shifts to make ends meet. What was she going to do? Eddie would flip out when he found out. She could dip into her grandparents' estate savings, but if Eddie found out, it would be gone in a flash. He'd already cleaned out their joint account more than once to fuel his addiction.

The light turned green. Two more turns and she'd be home. Ten more minutes, tops. Not that it mattered. It would all be her fault, anyway. It always was. Business slowing at the diner? Her fault. Rising grocery prices? Her fault. Eddie's failures? Everything was always her fault.

One turn. Five more minutes. She didn't want to go home. Not where her heart was anymore.

At the last stoplight, she wiped another tear from her tired, bloodshot eyes. She was bone tired, as Grams would've said.

"I miss you, Grams."

She could use a cup of Grams' special tea and a side of no-nonsense wisdom. She pictured the old porch swing and the long afternoons spent daydreaming. Never had she imagined her life turning out like this.

In the rearview mirror, her limp brown hair framed dull brown eyes. Her face, pale and drawn, looked older than it should. The silver lining? She'd lost a few pounds. Her cheekbones were more defined now. The scar along the side of her face from the car wreck that claimed her parent's lives as a child was faint.

She pulled into the driveway. Oscar, her black-and-white mixed-breed dog, barked from the backyard. Emily managed a weary smile as his big eye peeked through a knothole in the fence. Her rescue pup. She'd feed and walk him later, then scratch behind those big black ears until he did his little paw tap.

Still, she sat in the car, unwilling to go inside. She thought again of Grams. Of safety. Of the good times with Daniel and Glinda. Her friends. "Run away to the coast," the billboard whispered again.

Her phone rang. She looked at the screen and smiled. Noah Devereaux.

"Noah," she said. "How are you?"

"I'm good," he said. That voice. Deep, familiar. Comforting, but a little more ragged than she remembered. "And you?"

How was she? Wasn't that a loaded question? "I'm hanging in there," she said.

"I'm calling about the memorial for Ben next month. Carly, Joey, and I are reopening the old bait shop. We're turning it into Snapper's Bar and Grill and throwing a grand opening spaghetti cook-off. We'd love for you to come. Everyone's going to be there."

Carly and Noah's younger brother, Benjamin, had died in an oilfield accident the year before. Emily's eyes stung at the memory. Snapper, they'd called him, for his quick wit and biting comebacks. Noah had stood so stoic in his dress blues, fresh from his last tour in Iraq. Her heart had broken for all of them. Carly standing quietly beside him. All her vivaciousness dim.

"Of course I'm coming," she said. Maybe she was running away to the Gulf Coast. She thought of the cash tips stashed in her bra. Eddie would have to touch her to get them, and it had been a long time since he'd bothered.

"Glinda said you can stay at the Redbird Inn since Grams' place needs some work. She has some cabins available. While you're here, we can walk through the house and see what needs fixing."

Emily leaned back against the headrest and closed her eyes. "That would be wonderful."

"That's great, Em."

Her breath caught at the sound of the old nickname. "Me too."

"Bye, Em."

"Bye, Noah."

It was time. No more delays. She opened the door and stepped inside.

Eddie's snoring filled the dark house. She flipped the light switch. Nothing. The clock on the microwave was blank.

"What the hell?" she muttered. She was sure she'd paid the bill. Her stomach churned as she looked up the number for the electric company.

While waiting on hold, she surveyed the wreck of a kitchen. Beer bottles like bowling pins. Trash overflowing. Takeout boxes stacked like a tower. The place smelled like Eddie. Old beer and lost dreams.

"I'm sorry, Ms. Breaux," the voice finally said. "The check was returned for insufficient funds. You'll need to pay the past due balance plus a reconnect fee."

"Thanks," she said, and hung up.

She could rescue them. Again. Use her tips to pay the bill. But no. Not this time.

She walked to the bedroom and pulled out a suitcase. A few changes of clothes. Toiletries. Then Grams' Bible.

She flipped to her favorite verse:

*"Have I not commanded you? Be strong and courageous. Do not be terrified; do not be discouraged, for the Lord your God will be with you wherever you go."–Joshua 1:9*

At the bottom of the page: a series of numbers. Grams' savings account. Her secret cushion.

She scanned the room. What would she take? A wedding photo sat on the nightstand. Once, it had meant something. Now, it mocked her. That smile. That girl. Gone. She was twenty-one then. Now she felt fifty-one.

She left the photo behind.

Instead, she grabbed the group picture from that last summer in Bon Chance. The one with the rabbit ears and the sun in their smiles. That was the girl she wanted to be again.

She placed the photo gently in her suitcase. Bible on top. Tears threatened, but she held them back.

One last look.

She crept down the hall. "Sleeping Beast" snored on the couch.

"I am no jackass." She threw the notice on his round belly and walked out the door.

# Chapter Two

"Are you scared, Noah?" eighteen-year-old Emily asked. "Nah," he said. "It's just boot camp."

"But after that? Where will you go?"

"Wherever they send me, I guess."

Emily stared down at her bare feet, dangling over the edge of the pier above the murky Gulf water. Bon Chance had been her home since her parents had been killed in a car wreck.

Since then, Noah had been her best friend, and soon, her hero. He was leaving to join the Marines, and she'd be leaving for the University of Lafayette to study hospitality.

Both were going to see the world. Get out of the small town. They wanted something different from the oilfield and office jobs that everyone else had.

Cajun music from a beach bonfire mingled with the soft crash of waves against the pier. Tonight was their going-away party. Noah would leave in two weeks. Emily would follow shortly after.

"I already have a campus apartment," she said. "Grams and I have been getting it ready. She and Glinda even made a quilt in the school colors."

"What about you, Em? Are you scared?"

"A little," she said. "It's all going to be so new. New people, a new place. I'll be on my own."

"You'll be okay," he said simply, reaching out to hug her tight to his side.

"I hope so."

"Noah! Emily!" Both turned toward the beach as they heard their names called. It was Benjamin, Noah's younger brother, followed by Gabriel, Ryder, and Grace.

"Over here!" Noah called back.

Benjamin jogged down the pier. "Grams and the folks are looking for us. Picture time. We need to find Carly and Joey, too."

Carly was Noah's younger sister, and Joey was her best friend. The two of them rounded out their circle of friends. The Boonies, they called themselves after Bon Chance and living in what they considered the boonies. Carly had given them the name after watching an 80s movie about a group of kids who had gone treasure hunting. They had done their own fair share of treasure hunting, spending hours of their summer looking for Jean Lafitte's treasure, reported to be hidden somewhere in their area of the Gulf of Mexico.

"There's no telling where those two snuck off to," Noah muttered.

"We know," Benjamin said, rolling his eyes.

Noah stood and offered a hand to Emily. "Did you check behind the bait shop?"

Sure enough, muffled coughing gave away Carly's location. She and Joey were hidden behind the shop, sharing a bottle of cheap wine and an even cheaper cigarette.

"Carly, why do you still try to smoke?" Joey teased. "You sound like you're about to hack up a lung."

"Shut up, Joey," Carly wheezed, flicking the cigarette into the water.

"The grown-ups want a group photo," Benjamin announced. "Last summer together and all that."

*"Let's get it over with so we can get back to celebrating,"* Carly said, grabbing the wine and tucking it back into its hiding place under an old tarp.

*When they arrived at the makeshift stage, Carly, Emily, and Grace took spots on the edge, their skinny legs swinging. The guys stood behind them.*

*"One, two, three... say cheese!" Pops called out.*

*"Cheese!" they chorused.*

*The camera flashed, freezing them in time.*

• • • •

NOAH HUNG UP THE PHONE and took a long sip of coffee, absentmindedly patting Sadie's head. Emily was coming home.

He wondered how much she had changed. Back then, she'd been all limbs and angles, her eyes too big for her face. The last time he had seen her was at the funeral. And that had been a pain filled haze.

Noah checked the time and drained the cup. Emily had been the last call he needed to make. Responsibilities completed for now, he needed another run. Running was the only thing that seemed to keep the anxiety attacks at bay. Maybe the endorphins cancelled out the panic.

The fall morning was cooler than usual, so he went to the closet to grab a hooded jacket. His stomach heaved when he saw the dress blues in the back. He took a deep breath and bent over, his gaze falling on the footlocker. He'd buried it in the back corner of the closet, like he'd tried to bury the memories of a war that still haunted his dreams.

He hesitated, then pulled it out and placed it on the bed. When he opened it, the scent of sand and sweat and sun hit him like a ghost.

He pulled out the locker and carried it to the bed. Sitting down beside it, he opened it up and pulled a packet of letters out. He ran fingers over his younger brother's familiar scrawl. Benjamin and Carly had written letters every week while Noah was in Iraq. Benjamin's brief letters were all about fishing and football, Ben's two loves. Carly's were pages long, full of local gossip, and who she was in love with that week. They sent the occasional picture, and care packages from home full of baked goodies from Glinda and Grams. Daniel, Pops' best friend and fishing buddy, sent smokes and playing cards.

He looked down at the letter shaking in his hand. Noah hadn't smoked a cigarette in three years, not since leaving the "sandbox", as they had all called it.

*I could use a cigarette now.*

He inhaled a deep breath and closed his eyes against the pain.

*It should've been me. Not Benjamin.*

Sadie rested her head on his knee, a quiet anchor in the storm.

"Wanna go for a run, old girl?" he asked.

Her tail thumped in reply.

Noah smiled and stood. He paused at the door, looking once more at the photo of the Boonies on the nightstand. Noah stopped before walking out the door and turned to look at the picture. Smiling sadly, he closed the door.

• • • •

EMILY'S MIND DRIFTED as the miles ticked away. It was a beautiful fall afternoon, and the sun was a welcome warmth on her pale face. Having worked the night and early morning shifts for so long, she had forgotten what the sun felt like. A light breeze from the open sunroof blew her hair around her face. She tuned to a rock station and turned up the volume. No sad country songs today.

She was headed home. But what would she do when she got there?

*One step at a time.*

"Don't go borrowing trouble," Grams would've said.

She remembered the drive from Lafayette after the accident that had taken her parents. Pops had the Cajun music channel on. The lively sounds of the accordion contrasted the somber mood in the late model Ford. Years later, Emily was making the move again. Again, it was with little more than a few clothes and prized possessions.

Driving south through the small towns of south Louisiana, memories flashed like the faded yellow dashes on the highway. The excitement of summers. The long days of playing on the beach, fishing, campfires at night. When vacation was over and her parents went back to Lafayette, she had always stayed for the rest of the summer with her grandparents. After her parents died, she moved in with them permanently. It was then in Gram's kitchen that Emily developed a love for cooking. She'd spent many hours in that old kitchen with Grams. Grams had taught her how to make a roux from scratch.

"No roux in a jar for me no, cher," Grams would tell Emily. Emily would stir with that old, stained wooden spoon for so long; sometimes she thought her arm was going to fall off.

Emily smiled at the memory. How long had it been since she'd made a gumbo?

Too long.

As she neared Bon Chance, she rolled down the windows. Oscar leaned his head out, ears flapping, tongue lolling.

Emily's heart sank when she pulled up to her grandparents' house. A blue tarp fluttered on the roof. Plywood covered the windows.

She leashed Oscar and walked up the steps. She stood there staring at the door, afraid to go in. Afraid of what she'd find.

Emily sat down on the top step of the porch. Petting Oscar, and ignoring her growling belly, she looked out across the front yard. How many times had she sat there as a teen? Waiting for Noah, or watching the stars, or daydreaming about the future?

A truck pulled up to the mailbox. It was Noah. The years hadn't changed him much. He had a sharp, strong jawline, the same as his cheekbones. A slight shadow of a brown beard and the curve of a smile softened the look. Made him more human than Adonis. And a far cry from the military man she had seen during her last visit.

He enveloped her in a hug as he met her on the porch. Emily relished the comfort of the simple hug.

"You're early," he said, smiling.

She stood. "Couldn't stay away."

"You okay?" he asked.

"I will be."

He cocked a dark eyebrow in question. "You'll let me know if you need anything?"

"I will."

"It's good to see you again, Em."

"You too."

She watched him drive away, then turned to Oscar.

"Come on, boy. Let's go check in."

The Redbird Inn, like everything else in Bon Chance, was only a short drive away. Owned by her grandmother's best friend Glinda for as long as Emily could remember, it was a place Emily knew well. Within a few minutes, Emily was pulling into the driveway. Like most houses in the area, the main house was on posts to prevent flood damage. There was a huge front porch at the top of the stairs and the door painted a cardinal red that suited the Inn's name. Two huge hound dogs pounded welcoming tails on the wooden porch as she walked up the stairs.

An older, speckled man answered the doorbell.

"Hi, Daniel."

"Emily, come on in! We weren't expecting you until next month. You hungry? Glinda, I brought you a visitor!" Emily followed him into the kitchen area of the Inn where Glinda spent her time, if she wasn't outside tending her yard.

"Daniel, this is no visitor!" Suddenly, Emily was enveloped in a bear hug. "Lord, girl! How we've missed you here! How are you doing? How is your Grandparent's house? You stopped by there?"

"It's going to take a bit of work," Emily said.

Glinda said, "It would make me so happy for you to be here. I just loved your grandma. I miss quilting with her! I still have some of our quilts in the guest rooms. Come on now. Daniel, you go get her bags. We'll get her set right up. Have you eaten?"

"Not yet," Emily said.

"Well, I'll tell you what. Let me make you a plate, and then we'll get you settled.

Looks like you haven't slept in forever. Girl, you got bags under your eyes bigger than my gumbo pot. Stay right here. I'll be back."

Glinda returned with a covered dish and led her outside and to a small raised cabin. It had steps that led up to a deck that surrounded the front. They climbed the few steps and Glinda opened the door and stepped aside, letting Emily in first. The cabin smelled like lemon oil and sea air; clean and salty.

The living room and kitchen were open. A small island with a sink separated them. A worn brown sofa with huge, hideous orange flowers and matching love seat flanked each wall by big windows. Despite the outdated and dark furniture, it was bright and sunny.

"Do you like it?" Glinda asked.

"I love it."

"It's yours for however long you need it. There are pots and pans, silverware, and all of that in the kitchen. If you want to come for breakfast, it's at eight and I'd love the company. Towels and sheets are in the closet in the bedroom. It's your basic furnished camp."

"Thanks. For everything."

"Not a problem. We take care of each other. It's what Grams and Pops would've done."

Emily felt tears well up, and, embarrassed, looked away. Glinda took that as a cue to leave.

Daniel appeared, Oscar in tow, "This big guy didn't want to be left, so I brought him first." Emily took the leash from

Daniel and walked the dog around the cabin. When she came back around, Daniel was walking back down the steps.

"I left your bags in the living room. I'll let you put your things where you want them."

"Thank you so much, Daniel," she said.

"Not a problem. I'm going to head out now."

She looked around the new place, smiling as Oscar sniffed at these new surroundings. It was definitely tiny. But how much room did they need, anyway? This morning she'd had three bedrooms, two bathrooms, a big kitchen, and a backyard that constantly needed attention. Tonight, she had half that space and the gulf for a front yard. She still had a husband, but that could be fixed.

"One thing at a time," Grams always said.

She walked through the kitchen, running a hand across the cheap laminate counter. It was smooth. And clean. She opened the cabinets, looked at the simple silver pots and pans that shone like the treasures they were. Touching a small pot, relishing the feel, she thought of the cooking that could be done in this room. While this sauce or that chili simmered on the stove, she could devour a book outside on the small deck.

After a walk-through of the rest of the small cabin, she ended up in the small bedroom that faced the Gulf. Painted a blue that matched the sky, it was Spartan in its simplicity. All it had was a bed, a dresser with a mirror, and an open closet with two abandoned white plastic hangers. The bed was covered with clean and crisp white sheets. A handmade quilt lay on top of that. Emily recognized it as one of Grams' favorite patterns. She and Glinda must have made this one. Emily lay on top of it, stretching out, crossing her arms above her head. She took a deep breath. Slowly, a smile spread across her face, her first genuine smile in a long time. She closed her eyes, saying a silent prayer of thanks.

One tear rolled out, then another.

For now, she was home.

# Chapter Three

*Where am I?*

Opening her eyes, Emily had a moment of disorientation. With consciousness came memory. She had left Eddie. In one day, she had moved out, quit a job, and landed in a new, but familiar place.

She stretched, savoring the quiet. Only the occasional call of seagulls interrupted the morning stillness. Oscar roused from the blanket she'd tossed on the floor and padded over to the bed, resting his head beside her with a soft thump of his tail.

Grabbing her phone from the nightstand, she sighed at the screen: three missed calls and two voicemails. All from Eddie.

She grimaced as she listened.

"Where are you? Why didn't you come home? Are you with someone else?" he ranted in the first.

"I will find you, Emily. And when I do..." he growled in the second. Not the first threat, but soon it would be the last.

*He'll have to find me first.*

She rolled out of bed, slipped on her shoes, and grabbed Oscar's leash. He was already bouncing with energy. They stepped out onto the steps and into the morning air. One whiff of salt and sunshine, and she was instantly transported back to summers spent here with friends and family.

The beach was mostly deserted. Only one older houseboat bobbed off the pier. The fishing boats had already gone out.

Oscar tugged toward the pier, where a small blue crab skittered along the wood. He dropped into a playful crouch, barking. The crab raised its pincers in warning. Oscar leaned

17

closer and yelped when it pinched his nose. Then turned and promptly peed on it.

Emily laughed, really laughed, for the first time in longer than she could remember. She tilted her head back, letting the sound out with the sea air. A silent thank-you drifted skyward.

Oscar barked again. A man was jogging down the beach with a large German Shepherd. Tall. Broad shoulders. Close-cropped hair.

Noah.

Her heart did a slow flip.

Lowering her eyes, she saw a tattoo of a rooster with the words "Semper Fi" scrolling above his heart. That hadn't been there when they were young.

"Mornin', Emily," he said, breath slightly winded. "I'd hug you but..." he gestured to his sweat-soaked chest.

"That's quite alright," she said, laughing.

"This is Sadie."

Emily leaned down to pat the dog's head. "Hello, Sadie."

Straightening, she asked, "How are you doing?"

"I was about to grab coffee. Want one?"

"Where?" Her stomach perked up. Coffee sounded divine. "Follow me."

He led them to the houseboat. It had a wide front deck and a smaller one on the back. Sea-blue railings gave it a cozy, nautical vibe.

"Let's sit on the deck and watch the world go by."

"Okay."

Oscar began tugging impatiently on the leash.

"You can let him off. Not much traffic right now. Sadie'll keep him in line."

"You're sure?"

"I'm sure."

Emily unhooked the leash. Oscar took off like a shot, barking wildly. Sadie was right behind him.

She followed Noah onto the deck. He pulled up a white rocking chair with sun-bleached cushions, then disappeared inside. The scent of brewing coffee soon followed.

"You want anything while you wait?" he called.

"Nah, I'm good."

She brushed hair from her face, unsure what to say. The silence stretched, but not unpleasantly.

"I think it's ready," he said, returning with two mugs.

He handed her one that read "Life's A Beach," his own said "Semper Fidelis." As their fingers brushed, she caught the faint scent of his cologne—woodsy, clean, undeniably masculine. Her stomach fluttered.

"Cream? Sugar?"

"Cream, please."

He returned with a small container.

"Just yesterday, I was the one bringing people coffee," she said with a smile.

"Still in Lafayette?" he asked, settling into a chair beside her, leaving just enough space.

"Yeah."

"Finish school?"

"No." She didn't elaborate. "What about you? What are you doing?"

"I'm building houses now. Contracting. I help Glinda with repairs."

That explained the muscles. Eddie had started to resemble the underbelly of a large fish, all blubbery and pale. And after a night of drinking, he smelled about the same.

"You okay?" Noah's whiskey-brown eyes searched hers.

"I'm fine. Thanks for the coffee."

"Thanks for the company. The quiet's nice, but so's a little conversation."

"How's Carly?" she asked.

"She's hanging in there. Snapper's is keeping her busy, as well as planning the cook off. She's in Biloxi right now. Want another cup?"

"Sure. I'm gonna check on Oscar."

Oscar and Sadie were harassing the sea gulls resting on the rocks. The gulls looked entirely unbothered. Satisfied, she returned. A fresh cup waited on the table.

Oscar came bounding back, tongue lolling. He jumped up, nearly toppling her chair.

"He's a handful, but he makes me laugh. So I keep him around."

They rocked in silence. The sea breeze and the creak of wood were like a lullaby.

"I've missed this place," she said.

"Why'd you stay away?"

She dodged the question. "All the storm repairs keeping you busy?"

"Always. There's always something to fix. This place, too." He motioned to the boat. "Been fixing it up."

A shiny black truck pulled up. Oscar barked once and bolted toward it.

"Sit," Noah said softly.

Oscar stopped. Sat.

Emily stared. "How'd you do that?"

"Picked it up in the service."

"What are you, the freakin' dog whisperer?"

He just smiled.

She almost asked more, but let it go. Everyone had off-limits topics.

"One more cup?" he asked.

"Sure, but I'll take it to go, if you don't mind. I haven't been to the store yet."

He stepped inside. She leaned back and closed her eyes, letting the quiet sink in. This wasn't Lafayette. No horns. No shouting. Just the sea.

He returned with a steaming mug.

"I need to get back and settle into my place. Get groceries." She smiled. "My place. I like the sound of that."

"We'll have to do this again."

"We will."

She leashed Oscar and walked away, coffee in hand, a smile on her face.

Yesterday she'd been stuck in traffic, dreading going home to a man who didn't love her. Today, she was sipping coffee beside the ocean, talking to a man with calloused hands and kind eyes.

No fairy tale, maybe. But it felt like the beginning of something better.

• • • •

NOAH WATCHED HER GO, hand absently resting on Sadie's head.

He knew who she was the moment he saw her on the beach. Emily Breaux hadn't changed much. She wore the look of someone life had worn thin. He recognized it. He saw it in the mirror every day.

She was still beautiful. Still carried herself like she didn't know it. He'd seen the scar she used to hide behind her hair. Noticed how thin she was. Glinda would fix that. He wondered how long she was staying. There was a reason she left Lafayette early.

He'd helped tarp the roof at her grandparents' house after the hurricane. Couldn't stand to see it fall apart.

She stirred something in him. A feeling he hadn't known in years. Not since he came home from Iraq. He hadn't dated seriously. One-night stands left him emptier than before.

But Emily, with her fragile strength and cautious smile, felt different.

Dangerously different.

# Chapter Four

Walking into the old grocery store, Emily smiled. For the first time, she was buying groceries just for herself. Whatever she wanted, she could buy. Well, maybe not whatever, thinking of the small stash of cash. But she didn't have to think of anyone else. Just Oscar, who was content with kibble and a few table scraps here and there.

She pushed the ancient cart down aisles that still had prices stamped on the products. She didn't have any idea what to buy. Knowing she wanted a *sauce piquant* for dinner, she needed to get the ingredients for that. Coffee definitely. Community coffee, her favorite. Maybe since it was just her now, she'd buy the whole beans. She frowned, no grinder.

She roamed up and down the aisles, picking up this and that. Considering, then putting some things down and placing some in the basket. She put her favorite peppermint tea in the basket, along with honey, coffee, and cream. She had thought about chicken and noodle soup, but decided to make homemade soon. A big loaf of wonderful smelling fresh French bread, her favorite cheeses, summer sausage, a big bag of Jelly Belly jelly beans, and a bottle of white wine completed the purchases.

She was still smiling as the items rolled down the conveyor belt.

"Emily Thibodeaux?" the older woman behind the register asked. It was Nellie. Nellie had worked at Prejean's Grocery for as long as Emily could remember.

"It's me."

"It's so good to see you. It's been awhile."

"Yes, it has. It feels good to be back."

"Well, stop back in and visit with us when you can," Nellie said.

"I sure will, Nellie."

Emily took the few bags from the cashier and cradled them like the treasures they were. She was still smiling as she walked out the door and into the waning sunlight.

...

Back home in the comfort of the small kitchen, Emily grabbed an onion from the red mesh bag and set it on the cutting board. The phone rang, and she jumped. The knife slid, and she cursed, almost slicing a finger. She looked at the caller ID, but already knew who it was.

Eddie.

Should she pick it up? And if she did, what would she say? What could she say? And what would he say? Did she want to deal with that?

She answered, "Hello, Eddie."

"Where are you, Emily?" His voice slurred, thick with anger."

"Don't worry about it, Eddie."

"The electric's still off," he snapped. "It's a damn sauna in here."

"I'm sure it is."

"You never think about anyone but yourself."

She hung up the phone and turned it off

"You're right, Eddie. I am thinking about myself. For once."

She took the knife and sliced off the end of the onion. How Eddie had complained the last time she cooked. How long did it take to cook? Where's the meat and rice? My mom never cooked like this.

She sliced off the other end of the onion. She peeled off the papery outside layer and tossed it in the garbage. If only Eddie could be tossed away as easily. She wished she didn't feel as fragile as the skin she'd just discarded. She wanted to be strong.

Her eyes burned as she cut the onion in half. She didn't know if it was from the onion, or the sting in her heart.

She put her hand over the pot to test the heat, noticing that it did not seem to be getting hot.

"Ah, come on," Emily said in frustration. The stove would not warm up. The onions were cut and waiting. But the stove was not co-operating. She checked the plug. It was plugged in. She tried again. Waited a few moments, then stuck a hand over the burner. Still no heat.

She would have to call Glinda.

*Damn.*

Glinda would call Noah.

*Damn. Damn.*

Noah would be in her house.

*Damn. Damn. Damn.*

Did she really want to cook? She didn't want Noah in her house. Not now. She didn't want any man in her space. Maybe microwave something? Maybe make a plate of cheese and bread? She looked at all the onions she had just cut up. She had to deal with it. How bad could it be? It was Noah?

She turned the cell phone back on.

More missed calls and texts from Eddie.

She'd deal with that later. She still needed to go to the cell phone store and change her number. The last thing she needed, besides Noah in her kitchen, was Eddie finding her. She had no intention of letting Eddie know where she was. She needed to get her home in order first.

She dialed Glinda's number.

"Glinda?"

"Yes?"

"Ever have any problems with the stove here?"

"No? Something wrong?"

"Um, no. I think I got it. Sorry to have bothered you."

"No problem. You sure you got it?"

"Positive."

*Damn.* What was she going to do now?

How many times had she had to fix a leaky faucet or creaky door at the house with Eddie? He'd never been able to fix anything. Opening beer bottles had been about the best he could do.

She took a deep breath and grabbed her laptop, thankful for the free Wi-Fi and Google.

After a quick search on the internet, she found a troubleshooting checklist.

"Check breaker," she said aloud.

"Figures. It *was* an electric stove." She went to the bedroom where the breaker box was and laughed at what she saw. The stove had simply blown a breaker. She clicked it back into place and went back into the kitchen and started cooking. She had fixed it. No Noah involved.

She was adding the tomatoes when there was a knock at the door. She had forgotten to call Glinda back and tell her she'd fixed it. It had to be Noah.

And it was. Noah stood on the porch, holding a small yellow toolbox.

"Glinda called me. She said you were having a problem with your stove?"

He came in and instantly she felt his presence in the small space.

No men allowed. Except Oscar. And a dog didn't count.

"I fixed it," she said, smiling proudly. "It was a breaker."

"A breaker, huh? Mind if I just check it out since I'm here?"

Yes, she did, but to say so would be rude.

"Go ahead," she gestured toward the kitchen, still standing behind the door.

When he entered the kitchen, she kept a safe distance, crossing to the living room while he pulled out the stove. This was one time she didn't like the tiny size of this temporary home.

He looked at all the connections, whistling a popular Cajun song while working. She watched as he frowned a couple of times, dark brow furrowing up. The muscles in his arms flexed under the short-sleeved white shirt. Emily took another protective step backwards, bumping into the sofa.

"Seems to be fine. Let me check that breaker," He dusted his hands on his jeans and headed to the bedroom.

Noah. Was. In. Her. Bedroom.

After a quick examination of the breaker box, he was back in the kitchen.

"Thank you for coming over," she said.

"It's no prob. That's what I'm here for. Whatcha cookin'?"

"I'm making a *sauce piquant*."

"You know, I loved Grams' *sauce piquant*."

His smile tempted her to ask him to stay. To enjoy his company while they ate. It could be like old times. She thought of looking over the table while they ate, hearing his laugh like they had so many times in Grams' kitchen. Definitely tempting, but too scary to follow through.

"I'll save you a plate," she offered. Then she remembered the coffee he had shared. "Or you could come back in about an hour and a half. It will be ready."

Wait, did she just invite this man to dinner? Would he stay for dinner or just take a plate? Maybe he'd just take a plate and go.

"I'd like that." He looked as uncomfortable as she felt. He crossed his arms and uncrossed them, finally settling his hands behind him on the counter.

"An hour and a half, huh?" he asked.

"Yeah."

"I'll stop back in then. Leave you to finish up. And I'll get cleaned up."

"Sounds great."

He cocked his head at her as if trying to figure out her thoughts. Good luck with that. The man was too perceptive. And still in the kitchen.

Dinner with this man was not a good idea.

But what would be the harm in it? She always cooked more than enough, anyway. Might as well not let it go to waste.

No. No. No.

Dinner with Noah was not a good idea. Better to dine alone than deal with this complication. She would offer him a plate and send him on his way.

"See you soon," she said, opening the door.

"See ya."

She leaned against the door. This was going to be a problem. He was a mess, and so was she. They had no business being anything other than friends. But maybe that's all he wanted? But what if it wasn't?

Unsettled, she went back to the kitchen. She stirred the red sauce, gave it a little taste, added some more Cajun seasonings and stirred some more. Maybe the motion would calm her down. When it didn't, she went through the house, straightening throw pillows and blankets that didn't need it.

An hour later, the food was ready, but Emily was not. She winced when he knocked on the door.

This time, instead of a toolbox, he had a bottle of wine.

"Thought I'd grab a bottle to go along with dinner. Since you took the time to cook," he said.

Wine, he brought wine. He was staying. Damn. Thinking quickly, she grabbed two plates, "How about since it's a nice night, we eat out on the porch?"

"We can do that," he said. "I like that idea. I start to feel closed in sometimes in the house."

He was looking at the floor as if he didn't want to look her in the eye.

She put silverware on top of the plates she had grabbed and handed him one. She may not know what to say, but she knew how to feed someone. Grams had taught her that.

He shook his head when she waited for him to make a plate. "You first," he said. "And I'll bring the wine out. I brought an opener too. Didn't know if you had one or not."

"I don't know if I have one or not. I haven't completely rifled through all the drawers yet."

They filled their plates and seated themselves at the small metal table at the end of the deck. Noah quickly uncorked the wine and poured two glasses.

"This is very good," Noah said after taking a bite of the spicy tomato sauce.

"Thank you," Emily said. Eddie had never been one to compliment her food.

Emily sipped her wine, enjoying the warm liquid. The night had just a touch of chill to it. She looked at the fire pit. One night soon, she would gather some wood and build a fire.

Noah noticed her stare. "One drawback to living on a houseboat is no fires. And I love a good fire."

"Yeah, a fire on the boat might not be the best idea," Emily said with a grin.

Finished with the meal, Emily stood up to collect empty plates.

"Have a seat. I'll get these," he said, reaching out for her plate.

Emily's eyes widened.

"Okay." She definitely was not used to this. She sat back down and sipped some more wine.

"So this long story you were talking about earlier, does it involve a man?" Noah asked after he returned and sat back down.

"Ahhhh, it must. It figures," he said when she didn't answer immediately.

"Why do you say that?" she asked.

"People usually don't just pack up and run away from home for no reason. Usually, it's a bad relationship. Or a warrant. You a wanted woman?"

She rolled her eyes. "Oh yeah. That's it. I'm so wanted."

He chuckled. "You should be. Don't sell yourself short." Then, as if to change the subject before it got too real. "So, what are some of your favorite things to cook?"

"I make an awesome gumbo. I'm always trying new recipes. But, I haven't had much time for that lately. I've been working a lot."

Emily had never been much of a drinker, and during the busy last few months, if she had time to do anything, she slept. She could feel the wine loosening up tense muscles and easing nervousness.

"Busy woman," Noah said.

"I guess."

"Why were you working so much?"

"I wanted to save money to take business and cooking classes at the local technical school. I wanted to open my own restaurant someday."

"So what was the problem?" he asked.

"Another long story," she replied, unwilling to discuss Eddie or the lack of money issue.

"Ahhh. Okay. I see," he said, even though it didn't sound like it. He didn't press though, and for that, she was grateful. She did not need to be opening up and getting close to this man who had disaster written all over him. Actually, she probably had it written more on herself than he did, but that was beside the point.

Noah copied Emily's relaxed pose, stretching his legs out and leaning back in the chair. It was the first time she had seen him relax. Now, he looked more like the old Noah.

She sipped the last of the wine, covering her mouth as a yawn escaped. Noah's eyes may be closed, but that didn't mean he wasn't paying attention.

"Tired?" he asked.

"Sorry. Been a long couple of days," she apologized.

"No problem. I can understand that," he said, getting up to leave. She stood as well.

"Thanks again for dinner," he said. "It was very good."

"You're welcome. And thank you."

He stood there for a moment, uncertainty flickering in his eyes. Then, he stepped forward and gave her a one-armed hug that was warm, brief, and over too quickly. The scent of salt and cedar clung to him, and the strength in that single arm made her wish, just for a second, that he hadn't let go so soon. "I'll see you tomorrow." He started to walk away, then turned. "I'm thinking about going crabbing tomorrow. Wanna go?"

*No*, Emily thought. *Say no.* She needed to settle in. Unpack. Stay away from handsome men.

"Sure," she said. *Damn it.*

"Come to my place around sunup and we'll head out."

"Okay."

She watched him walk to the boat.

This was definitely going to be a problem.

# Chapter Five

The sun was barely over the horizon when Emily crossed over to Noah's houseboat. Oscar was straining at the leash, ready to go play with Sadie.

Noah had left the gate unlatched and he could see a light coming in through the galley window. She caught the rich scent of coffee in the air. Bless him.

She walked around to the sliding glass doors in the front. Noah smiled when he saw her and waved her in. His dark, sleep-rumpled hair fell against his forehead. He was shirtless, Emily found his bare chest almost irresistible. She slid the door closed and stood there, afraid to move further. She was afraid one-step would lead to two, and two would lead to her running her fingers through that rumpled hair.

"You can come on in," he said, as if reading her thoughts. "You wanna make yourself a cup of coffee while I shower?"

Noah. Shower. Not only was she motionless, she was now speechless. She nodded.

"Cool. I won't be long. I'm running a little late this morning."

"I'll be outside," she said. Outside with less temptation. Outside where there was no bed in sight. Outside where she couldn't hear the water run and have mental images that were way too tantalizing.

"Great," he said. He disappeared into the bedroom, leaving the door cracked just enough to send her nerves into a full sprint. She fled onto the deck. Only once she was outside, seated and pretending to breathe normally, did it hit her. She hadn't poured the coffee. "Seriously?" she muttered. She always drank coffee first thing in the morning. But apparently, a half-naked, dripping Noah short-circuited her brain.

Quietly, she slid the door back open. Sneaking in like a thief, she padded across the floor. Halfway through the room, she stopped and giggled. If he asked, she would simply say she'd needed more cream. She quickly poured coffee into the mug she now considered hers. She was taking a sip when he came out of the bedroom. The cup paused at her lips.

Sleep-rumpled Noah was half as tempting as wet, freshly showered Noah. She gulped the coffee down, wincing as it burned all the way down to her belly. *Good*, maybe that would kill some of the nerve endings that were reacting like crazy. At least he'd put a shirt on.

He crossed the room and joined her in the kitchen, his presence filling it as it had in her own small kitchen. Emily took an unconscious step back. She sipped the coffee in silence, slower this time.

"So, whaddya say? Ready to head out?"

"Sounds good to me."

"You wanna take a cup to go? I have a couple of mugs."

"That sounds great," she said.

He grabbed a couple of plastic travel mugs and filled them full of coffee. He handed her a mug, then grabbed a plastic bag out of the fridge and threw it in a small collapsible ice chest.

Within a few moments, they were all loaded up, dogs, ice chests, and crabbing gear. They drove to a place a few miles down the road. There were already a few people casting their nets and lines out along the piers. He pulled out the equipment and two folding chairs, and Emily followed him to a place away from the others.

It had been a long time since she had gone crabbing, but she was surprised at how much she remembered. She baited her line with a piece of turkey neck and dropped it into the water off the pier.

She was tempted to sit on the edge and dangle her feet but she had learned years ago not to do that. A hungry alligator had surfaced near her feet and nearly scared her to death.

The sun was warm on her face. She closed her eyes and smiled. Eddie and Lafayette seemed half a world away.

She felt a tug on the line. Slowly, slowly, she started pulling the rope out of the water. She laughed with delight as she saw the crab dangling from the bait. Noah was there with the net to capture and put in the bucket. She baited her hook with Noah watching. He nodded and smiled.

He held out a net. "I'm going to go see what I can catch. Let me know when you catch more."

She dropped the bait down into the water and sat waiting. She could hear the splash of Noah's net hitting the water and being pulled up again. Another tug and she snagged another crab.

"Noah!" she called. He pulled the net out of the water and grabbed the other net. He captured the crab and threw it in with the other one.

He plopped down beside her as she baited another hook. They were quiet. Emily would bring up the crabs, and he would net them.

They fished in silence until Noah went back to netting shrimp. Emily kept snagging crabs. Before long, they would have enough to boil.

The sun was now right above them. Emily pulled the sleeves of her t-shirt up to tan her zombie white skin. She checked the phone for the time. It had to be getting close to noon. They had been here for almost five hours now. She yawned. A nap would be incredible right now. Leaning back against the ice chest used as a makeshift back rest, she closed her eyes.

...

*She was at the inn. Noah was beside her. He reached out and pulled her closer into his arms. His chin rested on the top of her head. She was wrapped up tight in his arms until he turned her around. He kissed her forehead. He kissed her cheek. He kissed her nose. He leaned in to kiss her mouth.*

*"Emily."*

*Her blood ran cold as Eddie's voice came from behind her.*

*She turned.*

*Eddie sat there on the bench beside her like he'd never left. Like he belonged. Like he owned her.*

*"What do you think you're doing?" he asked, voice low and sharp as broken glass. "You think you can just run off and everything's gonna magically work out for you?"*

*She didn't respond. Noah stepped back, his warmth disappearing like mist in the sun.*

*"You really believe he's gonna stay?" Eddie's mouth twisted into a smirk that never reached his eyes. "You can't even hold your own life together. How long before he figures that out?"*

*Her throat tightened, but she forced herself to meet his stare.*

*Eddie leaned forward, eyes glinting. "You and me, we're the same mess. You don't get to pretend otherwise."*

She turned toward Noah, but he was gone.

...

Something tickled her nose. Without opening her eyes, she reached up to swat it away. Opening her eyes, she saw Noah dangling a piece of grass from his fingers. He'd been tickling her face with it.

"Sweet dreams?" he asked.

"Not really," she said, remembering the dream about Eddie. She could do without those kinds of dreams.

"You ready to go?" he asked.

"Actually, I am," she said. "I think I could use a nice long walk along the beach and a nap. And I still need to unpack."

"Gotcha. We'll get you home." He helped her to her feet. "We'll do something with these crabs and shrimp later. I'll clean them up tonight, and we can decide tomorrow. What do you think?"

"I think that sounds great."

...

Emily could see the rain approaching across the bay through the pale beige curtains. She loved this view. Anytime she wanted, she could open the curtains and stare out at the water. The sky was gray, the sun nonexistent. The waves were even gray.

Emily sat on the bed cross-legged thankful that she brought the bright pink fuzzy cotton Betty Boop pajamas. They fit her mood this morning, even though the stormy weather outside didn't. Inside, she was content, almost happy.

A suitcase lay open on the floor, along with the few other items she'd grabbed. She had thrown her mother's quilt, a dog-eared, stained cookbook, and the laptop in the car before grabbing Oscar.

She had left so many things behind. A bookcase full of treasured books. The photo albums on the coffee table. Perhaps she would return for those items. A few summers ago, she had scanned all the photos and saved them onto the laptop. If she never got the albums back, she could always reprint the pictures. An extensive music collection was on the laptop, too. Pop songs with catchy sing-along lyrics streamed from the computer's weak speakers. Now and then, she caught herself singing along while she unpacked. The stay may be temporary, but she still wanted to make it feel like home. Her home.

Emily grabbed the red, white, and blue quilt laying on top of the huge, beaten-up suitcase first. After her parents had passed, Grams had taken material from their favorite clothes and quilted Emily this blanket. After years of washing, drying, and covering Emily in comfort, it was faded and even worn out in some spots.

Emily folded it again gently. Where should she put it? Not on the bed. The quilt was wearing out. Time had done enough damage. Maybe the foot of the bed, just to drape off the end? No. Oscar tended to jump up there during storms. The plain wooden headboard? Perfect. She folded the quilt in half and gently draped it over the top.

Another of Gram's favorite bible verses was quilted at the bottom, floating above the small pile of pillows. *And now these three remain: faith, hope, and love. But the greatest of these is love. 1 Corinthians 13:13*. It reminded her she was loved, no matter what. She hadn't always had faith or hope, but her family had loved her. And here was proof. She touched the soft, worn fabric and smiled.

The various shades of blue denim were from her dad's jeans. An oilfield worker and fisherman, he had lived in beat up blue jeans. No fancy work clothes for him. White cotton from t-shirts dotted with oil smudges were from him as well.

The white flannel fabric with red roses was from her mother's favorite robe. An avid gardener with a spectacular green thumb, her mother had surrounded herself with flowers of all shades, sizes, and scents. Gardenia had been a favorite, and the smell always reminded Emily of her mother. She should plant some gardenia in Grams' garden if there weren't any there already.

What would her parents think of the mess her life had become? Her dad would find a way to make it better with a joke. Laughter, for him, had always been the best medicine. Emily hoped that the brown eyes she'd inherited would echo his one day. His laugh-lined eyes were a testament to a life well lived and enjoyed.

Her brown hair had come from her mother. How many times had Emily come home to find her working in the garden? With dirty smudges on her face? Enjoying the feel of the dirt under her hands, she had never been one to use gloves.

That quilt meant home. And now this was home. For however long she needed to stay. Emily climbed back into the bed to watch the water. There wasn't much else to do. There was a small television in the living room that caught a few local channels. It wasn't much, but Emily had never been one to watch television. She loved all the cooking shows, but couldn't catch any on that TV. Lost in thought, she'd rather listen to music this afternoon.

Two days ago, she'd been stuck, and now she was free. She flexed her legs out, glorying in the space. It was HER bed. HER House. She could run around naked if she wanted. She could listen to cheesy love songs. She could sing at the top of her lungs. She could pull a Risky Business and sing old rock in a t-shirt and socks. She could do ANYTHING she wanted.

She giggled.

Oscar looked up from his makeshift bed as if confused by the laughter. Lord knew there had been little to laugh about in the past few months.

For the first time, she was free to do whatever she wanted.

Freedom.

"I could get used to this," she said, climbing out of the bed. She took off at a jog, and slid through the living room in socks, true Risky Business style.

• • • •

NOAH JOGGED ALONG THE beach. The salty breeze lifted the ends of his damp hair, and the rhythmic thud of his sneakers against the sand mixed with the jingle of Sadie's tag against her collar. They rounded a bend, and Emily's little trailer came into view.

It was boxy and compact, one of those older models that had clearly been given a second life. Its white paint was faded in spots but still clean, with a hand-painted wooden sign hanging just below the front window that read *Sea la Vie* in bright turquoise letters. A set of wind chimes made from driftwood and tiny shells tinkled near the door, spinning lazily in the breeze.

He slowed his pace, giving Sadie a quick "heel." She fell into step, ears twitching at the sound of seagulls somewhere overhead.

Then he saw movement. Just a blur of color through the rain-blurred window.

Emily.

She spun past the front window. A white t-shirt flowed around, brushing against bare legs that moved with the unselfconscious joy of someone dancing alone.

He barely caught a glimpse. A flash of leg and a mess of brown hair swinging. But it was enough to make him grin. There was something about seeing her so unguarded and carefree.

He looked away. Fast. He wasn't some weirdo spying on her.

"Come on, girl," he murmured to Sadie, giving her a scratch behind the ears. "Let's get home."

By the time they got back to the houseboat, the light drizzle had turned into a steady rain. Sadie shook herself out as soon as they stepped onto the deck, sending droplets flying in every direction. Noah grabbed an old towel from the hook near the door and crouched to dry her off.

"You're lucky you're cute," he muttered, rubbing behind her ears. She licked his cheek in response.

Inside, he toweled off his own face and hair, still grinning like a fool. Emily, spinning around in her trailer like no one was watching, was now permanently imprinted in his brain.

Running through his contacts, he located her name and grabbed his phone. He hesitated for only a moment before he hit "call". He wondered if she would want to be disturbed.

She picked up after the second ring. "Hey," she said, a little breathless.

"Hello," he said, aiming for casual, and probably missing. "You got plans later?"

She laughed. "Depends. What's up?"

"I was thinking... crab boil. You, me, the dogs. Maybe a couple chairs and some cold beer."

She paused before answering, kicking his anxiety up a notch. "That actually sounds perfect. My place okay? I've got more yard, and I'm still trying to make it feel like home."

His smile deepened. "Your place is perfect. I'll bring the gear."

· · · ·

THE POT HISSED, STEAM rising in fragrant bursts as the boil simmered over the burner Noah had set up in the gravel clearing beside her trailer. The smell of Cajun spices drifted through the humid air, wrapping around Emily like a memory. It had been years since she'd been part of a boil like this.

From her spot on the porch steps, she watched Noah move around the setup with calm confidence. Then, cracked open a beer and handed her one. "To fresh caught crabs and fresh starts," he said, tapping his bottle gently against hers.

Emily smiled, the clink of glass sharp and comforting. "I'll drink to that."

A local radio station buzzed from his truck's open windows, the DJ's voice fading into a Cajun song that settled into the background. The dogs snoozed in the shade. Oscar curled tight near the steps, Sadie sprawled like royalty in the patch of grass beside the picnic table.

Noah leaned back against the truck, keeping his eye on the pot as if it were a ritual he'd performed a hundred times. "So... any thoughts about what's next? For you, I mean."

Emily stared into the pot for a moment, "I haven't let myself think about it in so long," she admitted. "Back in Lafayette, I was just... surviving."

Noah said nothing, and his quiet presence urged her to continue.

"I used to dream about my own place. Some sweet little bistro with mismatched chairs and chalkboard menus. But lately, that feels like too much."

She glanced at him, catching his easy nod.

"Maybe a catering business? Something smaller. More personal. I like the idea of creating something special for people. Weddings, birthdays, graduations. Celebrations."

"Bon Chance could use a good catering company. Most people hire out of New Orleans or Houma. But someone local, someone who understands the community... that's what folks want. Actually, I've talked with Joey about this a couple of times. He's not ready for it, but I think you are."

She blinked at the certainty in his voice. "You think?"

"I do." He looked over at her. "You've got the heart for it. That shows. And that sauce piquant was amazing."

A blush crept onto her cheeks as the compliment unexpectedly struck a chord, stirring emotions she hadn't anticipated. She looked down at her bottle, suddenly a bit self-conscious. But in a good way.

The boil finished, and together they drained it out onto the newspaper-lined table he'd set up. Corn, potatoes, bright red crabs, and shrimp tumbled into a glorious, steaming heap. Noah handed her a wedge of lemon, then took one for himself.

As they cracked shells and dipped bites into spicy homemade sauce, Emily let herself relax. This is what peace was like. The crunch of crab shells. The flick of buttered corn. The slow rhythm of a shared meal.

He told her more about his work. About how coming home after the Marines hadn't been easy. "I tried the regular jobs," he said, tossing a shrimp tail into a bowl. "Clocking in, pretending like I hadn't changed. But it didn't fit. I felt like I was watching my own life from the outside."

She nodded. "So you made your own way."

"Yeah. Took some time. Still figuring it out. Day by day."

They shared the last crab, fingers brushing briefly over the shell. Emily didn't pull away. She could've. She didn't want to.

The sun hung lower now, golden and thick, casting long shadows across the gravel. Emily leaned back in her chair, full and warm in more ways than one.

"I was planning to go to Grams' tomorrow," she said. "Check on the damage. See what's salvageable."

"I'll come with," he offered, no hesitation. "We'll take a look together."

She smiled. For the first time in a long while, she didn't feel like she was facing everything alone.

# Chapter Six

The rain was still lightly falling as Emily pulled up to Gram and Pop's. The grey backdrop only added to the sadness of the house. A light drizzle seeped down the broken windows and onto the chipped paint.

Her hand trembled as she unlocked the door and eased it open, grimacing at the protest of rusted hinges.

The sheets she had draped over the furniture were still mostly in place, but now dotted with brown water spots. Bits of beige ceiling plaster littered the floor where the roof had leaked. Several dark circles marred the ceiling above, with wooden rafters peeking through.

After Grams died, she had come down and packed up the important pictures and keepsakes, boxing them into plastic tubs and storing them in the attic. She hoped they were still safe.

She turned toward the kitchen, steeling herself. The old wooden door creaked, a sound like a sigh, as she pushed it open, and a wave of relief washed over her.

"Thank God," she whispered.

The kitchen had held up well. No leaks. No broken windows. The ceiling remained intact. Her eyes moved over the familiar red pepper accents painted onto white cabinets. She and Grams had painted them together after she got into ULL. The sun had bleached the bright red to a dull orange.

The cast-iron pot used to make so many gumbos was still sitting on the stove. Emily was saddened at the amount of rust it had accumulated. It would need to be cleaned and seasoned again. But Emily was glad she had left it, at least it was here and not Lafayette.

Emily walked past the farmhouse style sink where Noah and T-Pop would clean the day's shrimp after a day of fun in the sun. Noah and Pops would clean the shrimp, and then she and Grams would cook an etouffee, a sauce piquant, or a gumbo. Sometimes, Grams and Pops would invite the neighbors over, if the catch had been good, and they'd tell jokes and play cards well into the night.

The layer of dust on the small kitchen island reminded Emily of rolling out homemade biscuits. To experience that scent one more time. Every Sunday morning after Mass, Grams had made homemade biscuits and gravy, sausage, and hash browns for breakfast. What she would give to spend one more morning in this kitchen with them. Emily's eyes watered.

She turned away and walked down the hall. She entered her grandparent's room first. Emily hadn't touched this room when she had come down here after the funeral. It had been too much to handle.

An old quilt still lay across the bed. She sat gently, picked up a pillow, and lifted it to her nose, but the scent of Grams' floral perfume was gone.

On the nightstand, a picture of her 21st birthday at Blue Dog's brunch smiled up at her. She set it down with trembling hands.

Beside it lay Grams' rosary, still nestled in its clear plastic container with the Virgin Mary on the lid. Emily twisted the cap off and was instantly wrapped in the scent of roses. A small smile broke through. She let the cold metal of the crucifix rest in her palm.

How long had it been since she prayed? Since she went to church? *Too long.*

Carefully, she coiled the beads back into the container and put it back on the nightstand.

The closet stood open. Grams and Pops' clothes still hung in neat rows. She would need to decide what to do with them. Maybe she'd make a quilt. Glinda could help. They could make one for each of them. Grams had been important to Glinda too.

She rose and crossed the hall.

Her old room greeted her like a time capsule. Posters of long-haired 80s rock stars blew kisses from neon backgrounds. Emily laughed softly at the absurdity of the hair and the memories they carried.

She drifted to her desk, gazing at photos tacked to the wall. High school pictures. A bleached-blonde mishap. Friends. Concerts. A younger version of herself.

Then, there was the picture of her and Noah. Pops had taken the picture after a fishing trip. At thirteen, she was thin as a rail, with a golden brown tan from the summer sun that matched the highlights in her brown hair. She was holding a red snapper that was almost as big as she was. She had teased Noah relentlessly that day, as it had been Emily that caught the biggest fish.

"Emily?"

She jumped at the sound of Noah's voice in the doorway.

• • • •

NOAH LINGERED IN THE hallway, watching Emily through the open door. She was still holding that old photo, the one from their fishing trip when they were kids. A smile tugged at the corner of her lips, and he caught a flicker of the girl she used to be.

She jumped slightly when he spoke. "Emily?"

She turned and gestured toward the photo, her voice soft. "Remember this?"

He stepped into the room. "Yeah, I remember. You were pretty annoying that day."

She laughed, "I'm sure I was."

"Man, that was a long time ago."

He glanced around the room. It was like stepping back in time. Posters, mismatched furniture, memories frozen in place. Some part of him had expected it to be empty, or changed.

"You ready to take a look around?" he asked, jerking his thumb toward the hallway.

They moved room by room, his eyes scanning for damage as she trailed close behind. He noted the sagging ceiling, the water-stained walls, the parts that would need gutting and reinforcing. But the bones of the place? Still good.

"It's not as bad as it looks, Em," he said when they stepped out onto the porch. The rain had finally eased to a mist. "Mostly cosmetic. No visible structural damage. Some elbow grease and you'll be back in this house in no time."

He glanced down at the old porch swing, its chain busted on one side.

"Remember that?"

She blushed and looked away. That was answer enough. One never forgot their first kiss.

"Hang on," he said, heading for his truck and toolbox. A few minutes later, he returned with a short length of chain and his toolbox.

She watched him quietly as he worked. With a few swift movements, the rusty chain was swapped out. The swing was reattached, feeling sturdy once more. He gave it a quick test.

"Come see," he said.

She sat gingerly, relaxing as the swing moved beneath her.

"Good job," she said.

"Good as new."

"Thank you."

"You're welcome."

"How much do you think it'll cost?" she asked.

He grinned. "The swing? That's nothing."

"No," she said with a smile. "The whole thing."

"I can work up an estimate tonight. Call you tomorrow. Just materials."

"That's too generous. I can't let you do that."

"Don't. Feed me, and we'll call it good. Fair trade."

"But..."

"Darlin', I loved Grams and Pops too. I wouldn't dream of taking money to fix this place up."

She studied him briefly, then nodded and extended her hand. "We have a deal."

Noah reached out and took it.

Her hand was smaller than he remembered, cool at first, then warming in his grip. A jolt of something familiar, something he'd buried deep, hummed under his skin. He didn't let go right away. Didn't want to.

Neither did she.

"Good," he said, a little rougher than he meant to. "Now, what do you have planned for tomorrow night?"

She eased her hand from his, and for a beat, he missed the contact more than he should've.

"Not much. Why?"

"Carly called earlier. She's coming in this weekend to work on Snapper's. We're all meeting at the inn tomorrow night. I can text you when I know what time."

"That sounds fun. I haven't seen everyone in forever."

"Great. I'll see you tomorrow."

"Yeah, tomorrow."

She turned to leave, heading toward her car, but pivoted back toward the house and bounded up the steps.

Noah tilted his head. "Forget something?"

"Grams' pot," she said, holding up the rusted cast iron like a prize.

He chuckled. "Now you can really do some cooking."

"Definitely. Well, I guess I'll see you tomorrow."

"Definitely," he echoed.

He watched her go, already looking forward to tomorrow.

She had left the door unlocked, so Noah did a slow walk-through of the house alone. He had grown up in this house as well. If he closed his eyes, he could hear Pop's booming and easy laugh. How many football games had he watched in this living room? Depending on the time, Grams would have finger foods, a huge meal, or both. The Super Bowl always garnered a feast to feed a small army. Or a few hungry men. How they had yelled at the coaches, the players, the referees, each other.

He walked to the kitchen. The other place he had spent many hours. He had no idea how many meals Grams had fed him.

"If you keep hangin' out here, I'm gonna claim you on my taxes, cher," she had joked, hitting him with a kitchen towel.

"I just can't keep away from you."

"Oh, you!" she would blush and hit him with the towel again.

He walked over to the bar where he had sat when he told them he had enlisted. Grams had smiled even though he could see the tears in her eyes.

"Oh, you're going to have such an adventure!" she had said.

"If you only knew, Grams," he said aloud toward the ceiling. "If you only knew."

He closed his eyes against the pain and walked out the back door, locking it behind him.

• • • •

"EMILY! COME HAVE SOME tea!"

Emily smiled at Glinda and waved back. "Coming!" She climbed the steps, her eyes briefly catching on the two familiar rocking chairs. After the walkthrough of her grandmother's house, she'd taken Oscar for a long walk along the beach to clear her head. Now, as they returned to the cabin, Glinda's voice rang out, stopping her in her tracks.

After a quick hug, Glinda said, "Take a seat, girl, and I'll get you some tea. Are you hungry? You look hungry."

"You don't have to go out of your way for me, Aunt Glinda. I can get some tea myself if you tell me where everything is."

"Nonsense. You sit."

Obediently, Emily took a seat. Surprisingly enough, Oscar did too, settling beside her with a sigh. She rocked slowly back and forth in the chair, her gaze drifting over the sparkling water. The movement, the breeze, the scent of salt. It all wrapped around her like a memory.

Within moments, Glinda returned with a tray. She set it down on the white wicker stand between them. Tea, a few croissants, and beignets. Emily's stomach growled on cue.

Glinda grinned. "Told you."

Emily smiled and reached for a croissant, deciding to save the beignets for dessert.

"So," Glinda said, pouring their tea, "tell me what you've been up to. Why are you here early?"

Emily hesitated. "Long story."

"I've got nothing but time," Glinda replied, smiling. "No tourists today, and nothing pressing."

Emily's eyes watered. She raised the glass of tea, and the familiar smell took her right back to Grams' kitchen.

"This is Grams'!" she exclaimed.

Glinda smiled, "Yes, it is. She gave me the recipe as a gift when I opened this place. I figured you could use a cup of it."

Emily's lip quivered. She closed her eyes and inhaled the scent of the tea. With every inhale of the cloves, the orange, and the cinnamon, she felt her grandmother's love.

She exhaled a shaky breath and looked at Glinda. "Thank you."

"You're welcome."

The tea warmed her throat, but the knot in her stomach remained. She set the cup down slowly. "I'm leaving Eddie," she said, the words louder than she expected.

Glinda reached over and squeezed her hand. "It's not something that can be fixed?"

"He's bleeding me dry. Drinks all day, takes my money, cleared out our joint account more than once. If he knew about Grams' money, he'd have taken that too."

Glinda's mouth tightened. "Then yes, you've got to do something. I figured something was wrong when he didn't come to Ben's funeral with you."

"There was no way I was bringing him here. I couldn't bear the embarrassment. He didn't want to come anyway."

"If he finds out about Ruby's money, he'll try to get it. And there might be nothing you can do to stop him once he knows. We'll ask Daniel if he knows a good attorney."

"Thanks, Glinda. I just want it over."

Glinda gave her hand a squeeze. "I understand, sweetheart."

She leaned back in her chair and sipped her tea. "You didn't happen to see Noah this morning, did you? I spotted him out on his run."

Emily nodded. "He met me at the house. Did a walkthrough with me."

Glinda smiled gently. "He's always been steady. Quiet, but dependable. Good man to have in your corner."

Emily gave a small smile. "Yeah. He offered to help."

"Well, that sounds like Noah." Glinda's voice was reassuring. "You know, whatever you need, we've got you."

"What I need now," Emily said, reaching for a beignet, "is one of these."

"Take two. And if you're still hungry after that, I'll cook you a real breakfast."

"I don't think I'll need all that. But thank you."

"You're very welcome, girl. It's so good you're home."

Emily paused, her throat tightening as the words settled in. "It's... it's good to be home," she said, her voice catching just a little.

Glinda reached over and gave her hand a squeeze. "You just breathe, baby. One step at a time."

Emily looked back toward the water. She already felt the sand's pull. "Aunt Glinda? Do you have any good books?"

"Of course I do. Come on inside. I'll set you up."

With a beach bag of books slung over one arm and a foldable chair under the other, Emily headed for the beach. She planted the chair, kicked off her shoes, and sank in. After all the rain, the sun was warm, the breeze light, and for the first time in a long while, she let herself just be.

She flipped open a book. A woman's journey. Finding herself. Finding balance. Finding love. The first two she could relate to. Love? Not so much.

She laid the book across her stomach and stared out at the waves. What did she want? A new job? Her own business? A life that wasn't about surviving, but actually living?

Her phone buzzed. Eddie. She turned it off.

Tomorrow, she'd see the others. She'd take one more step forward.

She closed her eyes, exhaled, and let that be enough.

# Chapter Seven

Leaving for the inn, Emily patted Oscar on the head, "Stay here, boy, I'll be back in a little bit. I'll bring you back something, I promise."

Oscar cocked his head sideways and barked. Emily took that to mean, "You better."

When Emily stepped out of the cabin, she instantly wished for a hoodie. The wind had picked up and there was a definite chill in the air that carried the scent of burning wood. Glinda must have started a fire.

Emily walked faster. Soon, she was knocking on the door.

Daniel opened the door. "Come on in out of the cold, *cher.* Where's your coat?"

"I didn't think I would need it."

"Come stand by the fire a minute, warm up. Glinda's got a spread laid out for dinner in the main room. She's been cooking all day."

"Daniel?" Glinda said, stepping out of the kitchen. "Is that Emily?"

"Yes," Daniel said. "We're getting her warmed up."

"Well, get her in the house!"

Emily followed Daniel into the main room, where a fire blazed in the fireplace. Little had changed in the room during the years Emily was away. The furniture had been updated. The front wall was still lined with small tables by French doors that had views of the bay. Customers of the inn frequently ate dinner there, or had drinks from the well-stocked bar that lined the opposite wall. Bookcases flanked the fireplace, filled with books that customers could read on the big, comfortable sofas and chairs. Emily's attention was drawn to the long table by the bar that held a bounty in covered silver serving trays heated by small burners. A stack of plates and silverware was on one end.

"Fix you a plate," Daniel said. "Do you want something to drink? I'll fix it."

"I'd love a glass of white wine," Emily said.

"Okay. I'll get it. You get you something to eat. Tonight is casual. Everyone will eat on their own time."

Emily took her time, taking the lids off each of the dishes, relishing the smells. Each unique spicy scent transported her back through time. There was seafood gumbo, jambalaya, red beans and rice, potato salad, French bread, and corn maque choux. Everything Emily had loved as a child. Emily decided she'd savor each one. She started with just a bowl of seafood gumbo and grabbed a thick slice of French bread to go with it.

Daniel was waiting at one table with her wine.

"That's all you got?" he asked.

Emily smiled, "For now." She stirred the gumbo, breathing in the heavenly smell of seafood and dark roux.

"This is incredible," she said after a sip. "I've missed Glinda's cooking."

"Actually," Daniel said. "Joey made that one."

"Joey?"

"Yes, he's turned into quite the cook. We keep telling him he should go to New Orleans or culinary school, but he doesn't."

"What about everyone else? How is everyone doing? Catch me up before they get here tonight. I've been so out of touch." Emily asked. Last time she'd seen them all was last year when Ben died. They had little time to visit then, and the promises they'd made to all get together soon were never kept.

"They're all coming. Noah got called on an emergency out at Ms. Jameson's house. He will be late." Daniel said. "Gabe should be here soon. He left Austin early this morning. He's been playing music there."

Emily smiled, remembering Gabriel, Grace, and Benjamin's garage band. They had spent many hours in Noah's parent's garage practicing and had gotten pretty good. Good enough to get gigs at some of the local bars. Grace had a singing voice reminiscent of a young Bonnie Raitt. Gabe just had a natural smooth way with the guitar. Benjamin had rounded out the group on the drums.

"Ryder and Grace are semi-roommates, so they're coming together."

Emily looked up from her gumbo. "Semi-roommates?"

"Ryder works in New Orleans and stays there during the week. He comes back here on the weekend. Hates the big town. If he's not off somewhere riding bulls, he usually comes home and chases women over in St. Andrew parish."

Some things never change. Ryder had always been the charmer of the group. The risk taker. He liked to drive fast, live fast, and chase fast women.

"Carly's been living in Biloxi, working at a casino, and living with her fiancé. They're set to tie the knot soon. A big blow-out in Biloxi, from what I hear from Glinda. His family comes from money. Joey went to pick her up so that they could get some stuff for the renovation of the bar on the way home. They'll be back soon as well. If they don't get into an argument."

"Grandma?" Gabriel called from the door.

"Gabriel?" Glinda emerged from the kitchen, arms open.

He hugged her. "Hi, Grandma."

She beamed. "How are you, baby?"

"I'm good. Ryder and Grace are right behind me. Carly too?"

"Yep. And Emily's here."

"Emily?" Gabe turned with a wide smile. "Well, hey there."

"Hi Gabriel."

"It's really good to see you." Emily eyed Gabriel over the bowl of gumbo. His curly light brown hair was swept back to the side. He had the face of a movie star, all angles and strong cheekbones. His deep green eyes were wide and expressive. The goatee was a recent addition. He wore a t-shirt from a local Austin night club and blue jeans. Still tall and skinny, he looked like a starving artist. A very handsome starving artist.

Emily sipped her wine and considered getting another bowl of gumbo, or jambalaya, or red beans and rice. She was eyeing the table when the door opened again.

A younger blonde walked in, followed by a dark-haired man of the same age. Carly and Joey. Grace and Ryder followed. Now everyone was here. Everyone except Noah. And Benjamin. Emily thought, wincing as her heart contracted. A year later, Ben's loss still hurt.

"If he thinks I'm going to sit here and be sad. He's got another think coming. He can be replaced," Carly said, flopping down on a couch.

"What are you talking about, *cher*?" Daniel asked, getting up from the table.

"Don't get her started," Joey said. He proceeded to the bar, poured himself a large shot, then prepared a drink.

"Drink this," he said, handing the drink to Carly.

"Well, isn't she a ray of sunshine?" Ryder said to Gabriel as they shook hands.

"Who is?" Carly said, blue eyes flashing, "You didn't just walk in on your fiancé, all fragrance de lecto."

"Do you mean *in flagrante delicto*?" Daniel asked.

"Yeah, whatever," Carly said. "I caught him naked."

"I'm assuming not alone," Daniel said.

"No! He wasn't alone. He had a woman! With shoes!"

Carly started pacing the room, grumbling to herself. Her blonde ponytail bounced behind her, flip-flops slapping on the hardwood floor. Emily caught the words, "douche bag and throat punch". The others left her alone, so Emily did too.

Joey fixed a drink and stood by the bar with Ryder and Gabriel. They exchanged handshakes. Grace quietly settled into a corner armchair, pulling her feet up.

"He was with another woman?" Ryder asked Joey. Joey nodded.

"Bastard," Ryder said.

"Agreed," Gabriel said. "What about the memorial?"

"He's not coming," Joey said.

"He better not," Ryder said.

"But to deal with opening the bar, the memorial AND this?" Gabriel said. "Yeah, he better not show up. Noah's going to blow a gasket."

Emily, feeling awkward, turned to look at the bookcases. She saw the framed copy of that last picture they took. The same picture she had packed. *We were so young. The world was our oyster. What had happened?*

"Emily?" Emily turned to see Ryder. Tall and lanky, with a devilish smile that matched his eyes. He wore a black cowboy hat, boots, and the shiny big belt buckle was from his latest rodeo win. She smiled and tucked the picture under her arm.

"Hi, Ryder," she said.

He enveloped her in a hug. "It's been too long. It really is good to see you again."

"Are you staying awhile?"

"It looks that way," Emily said. "Noah and I did a walk-through of the old house today."

"We can help you with that, too." Ryder said.

Joey appeared at Emily's side with a warm grin and a hug. "Glad you came. We've missed you."

"Thanks. It's good to be back," Emily said.

Grace moved in next, offering a soft smile and a hug of her own. "It's really good to see you again, Emily."

"You too, Grace. How have you been?"

Grace shrugged, her smile turning wistful. "Busy. The music scene in New Orleans is hopping. Tired, though. I'm going to walk Furby one last time and call it a night."

Emily nodded, suddenly aware of her own yawn creeping up. "I might do the same."

Joey caught it and grinned. "You turning in?"

"I think so."

"Come help us with Snapper's tomorrow? We'll catch up over beers."

"I'd like that."

"Good." He hugged her again. "It's good to have you home."

"Sorry I'm late," came a familiar voice from the entryway. It was Noah and suddenly her senses were on fire. All thoughts of going home disappeared. Hell, she wasn't even tired anymore.

She turned, heart thudding, and found him shrugging off his jacket. He looked worn from the day. His boots were dusted with dirt, a long-sleeved shirt fit snugly against his broad shoulders, and his hair was a little tousled from the wind.

"Go grab some gumbo," Daniel said, motioning toward the buffet table.

Noah gave a small nod, but his eyes lingered on her just a moment too long and Emily's cheeks flushed. He walked over to greet her.

"Hey," he said, his voice low.

Before she could answer, his attention flicked to Carly who was grumbling again.

"What happened with her?" he asked.

Joey followed his gaze. "Fiancé trouble. The kind that ends with thrown shoes and swearing. We'll catch you up after you eat."

Noah winced. "Damn."

"You want to join me?" he asked Emily.

"I would love to."

Emily tucked the photo she'd been holding back onto the shelf, right where it belonged. And being here with these people, she felt like she was right back where she belonged, too.

# Chapter Eight

C arly opened the door of the old bait shop with a flourish and a bow, despite her bloodshot blue eyes.

"Ladies and gentlemen, may I present the future Snapper's Bar and Grill."

Emily followed the group into the old building.

"So, Carly? Where do you want us to start?" Noah asked.

Emily looked around the old bait shop-turned-bar. Once the start of fishing trips with her dad, it was halfway to becoming Snapper's. Neon signs leaned against the wall, a pool table waited for players, and a dusty jukebox stood by the corner.

"We need to get the bar area ready. The cash register is there already. We have barware to clean and set out. It's there in those boxes by the liquor samples the distributor sent. Girls, we can clean and start decorating."

Emily watched as Carly walked through the building, talking to herself, "The jukebox works there. We have the pool table already. Do we need another? Need to check the bathrooms."

"I'm going to check out the kitchen," Joey said. "See what needs to be done in there. I'm sure it's a mess."

"Ryder, Gabe, you want to help me get the stuff out of the truck?" Noah asked.

"You want to help me find some stuff to clean with?" Emily asked Grace.

"Sure."

Soon, everyone was busy. Joey was in the kitchen. He had shooed everyone out, saying if it was going to be his domain, then he was going to be the one to get it ready. Carly was busy hanging new decorations she had picked up, including a "Coming Soon" banner. The rest of the guys were busy with hammers, saws, and whatever else they needed to finish the bar. Noah had brought the plans, and they had gotten to work.

Emily felt Noah's eyes on her as she swept the massive floor. She looked up and met his glance and blushed. He smiled at her and resumed working. Carly was a dictator and if she caught you not working, she found something for you to do.

Hours later, the group took seats at the bar. Carly handed out beer she had brought in an ice chest, and they took a moment to toast.

"To Snapper's!" Carly raised her bottle.

"To Snapper's!" everyone echoed.

Noah lifted his own with quiet reverence. "To Benjamin."

A hush fell, then they all echoed again, softer this time.

"To Benjamin."

The door opened, and a stranger came in. "Oh God," Carly said. "It's Cheech."

"Cheech?"

"That's what Joey and I call him. That's what he looks like. His real name is Charles. He's a local, a fisherman."

Emily glanced over. Sure enough, the man looked like Cheech from the Cheech and Chong movies. Same shaggy gray hair, same slightly narrowed and hazy eyes.

"Are you guys open?" he asked.

"Not yet, but come on in. You can play some pool," she said, and after that whispered to Emily. "He's harmless most of the time. He'll just ask you what your name is every time he comes in."

Cheech spotted Carly and came over.

"Hey, pretty lady. Carly, right?"

"Hi Charles," she replied. "Yes, it's Carly. And this is Emily."

"Oh hi, Emily," he replied with a chuckle. "So, Emily, do you smoke pot?"

Emily's eyes widened. "Um no."

"That's cool. Just thought I'd offer," he said, then walked off to the other side of the bar.

Carly laughed.

"That's one of our more colorful locals," Carly said.

"Yeah, I'd say. More like psychedelic," Emily said.

Carly laughed, "Yes, exactly. Man, I needed this. After yesterday."

Emily nodded her head, unsure of what to say, but knowing what Carly was feeling. It felt good to be surrounded by her friends. She watched as Cheech grabbed a beer from the ice chest, then went off to the pool tables to play a game by himself. He mumbled the whole time.

Ryder popped the top on a beer and came to sit beside them. His brown eyes traveled up and down her body, and he grinned. "So, you have a boyfriend?"

Emily looked over at Noah. He had taken a seat at the end of the new bar, and was sitting quietly, staring out into space, peeling the label off his beer.

"No," Emily responded. Technically, she didn't have a boyfriend. And he had asked nothing about a husband.

"Girlfriend?" he asked.

"No!" Emily's face flushed.

Carly smacked his arm. "You're embarrassing her."

"And?" Ryder asked, still smiling. He had a beautiful smile, a genuine smile that reached his chocolate brown eyes.

"Wanna get naked and throw potato salad, then?"

"What?"

"What? You don't like potato salad?" he smiled at her.

Emily smiled back, as his smile was contagious.

"Hey pretty ladies," Cheech was back. "Is the jukebox working? Wanna hear some music?"

"The switch is in the back. Play what you want," Carly said. "I like all kinds of music."

"Cool, man," He chuckled a bit, and then said. "I mean wo-man."

Cheech walked over to the stereo. Emily watched as he slowly shuffled through the stations. At his pace, they might hear music the next day.

"Well, will you dance with me?" he asked as a popular, fast country song came on.

"No. Maybe next time. I am not a good dancer. How about Carly?"

Carly, Ryder, and Joey laughed.

"No, she can't," Ryder said. "She's hopeless."

"He's right," Carly agreed. "Last time he tried to teach me; he kicked me in the shin."

"On purpose?" Emily asked.

"On purpose."

"I think I'll pass on the dance," Emily said, smiling.

"Okay," he looked at her again and smiled. "But let me know if you change your mind. About the dance or the potato salad."

"Will do," Emily said.

The country music faded and the strains of a popular Christmas carol came on. Emily looked at Carly.

"What the hell?" Carly asked. "It's October."

"Well, apparently for Cheech, it's Christmas time." Joey said.

*"I'll be home for Christmas."* wafted through the room.

"Sure you don't want to dance?" Ryder asked her. "It's a slow song."

She chewed her bottom lip and looked at Carly, who smiled back. "Go ahead."

"If I do, you have to dance too," Emily said, sure Carly wouldn't agree. She would be saved.

"Fine," Carly said. "C'mon, Joey." She grabbed Joey's hand. Emily groaned.

Ryder extended a hand, and Emily cautiously took it. The four of them walked to the small empty area in front of the jukebox. Emily stood stiffly in front of Ryder. He was a head taller than she was, so she stared at his shirt. She took a few hesitant steps and tried to follow him.

"Relax," he said. "It's only a dance. And I left the potato salad at home."

He respected her need for space and held her close, but not too close. He set a slow pace that was easy to follow. His hand rested on her hip. Her hand was on his shoulder. She found herself relaxing and letting herself follow him and the slow beat of the music.

"See?" he said. "You're doing fine."

As Ryder spun her gently, Emily felt something shift. Just for a moment, she wasn't a woman on the verge of divorce or the outsider. She was just a woman dancing

The music ended, and Ryder gave her a quick hug. "Thank you."

"That was fun," Emily said. "Thank you. I haven't danced in years."

"Then it's about time you started again."

"Maybe so," Emily said.

As they resumed their seats, Noah's eyes found Emily's, and she wondered what it would be like to dance with Noah again after all these years. She wondered what it would be like to hold him close. Her stomach fluttered. His eyes narrowed, and she foolishly wondered if he could read her thoughts. Nervously, she looked down, sipping the drink.

Noah left his spot at the end of the bar where he had been on the outskirts of the group, nursing a beer.

"I'm flirting with Emily here," Ryder said as Noah took a seat beside him, grinning and winking at Emily.

"Oh really? And how is that working out for you?"

"It's not," Ryder said. "She doesn't like potato salad."

Emily laughed and finished the drink.

"You want another one?" Noah asked.

She was tempted. Oscar, though, was probably ready for a walk.

"You guys staying here for a little while?" she asked.

Carly laughed, "More than likely."

"I'm going to go walk Oscar and come back," Emily said. Rather than sit alone at the house, she would come back and enjoy their company. A little laughter would do her good. She thought of the picture on the fridge. The picture of herself smiling. It was time to find that person again.

"Mind if I go with you?" Noah asked. "Sadie probably could use a break, too."

"Sure," she said.

"We'll be back in a bit," Noah said to the others.

"You want to meet me in front of my place?" she said to Noah.

"I can do that."

• • • •

EMILY JOGGED BACK TO the cabin, leashed Oscar, and returned to find Noah already waiting with Sadie at his side. Her heart gave a small, traitorous flutter.

"Ready?" he asked.

"Yep."

Noah saw Oscar straining at his leash, ready to run. "You can let him go when we get to the beach."

When they reached the beach, Emily unleashed Oscar. He and Sadie took off down the waterline. Noah and Emily walked slowly behind them. Emily wondered what it would be like to feel her hand in his and stroll down the beach.

Emily's cell phone started ringing, and she cringed. It had to be Eddie. Again. Should she answer? She looked at the caller id. Sure enough, it was Eddie.

She froze, thumb hovering. Just seeing his name made her stomach twist. By the time she decided against answering, the call had already gone to voicemail. When the message alert chimed, she pulled up his message. She turned her back to Noah as she listened.

"Em," Eddie said. "I'm sorry. Please answer the phone. I need to talk to you. I took care of the rent and the electricity. I got the money from my sister. Please call me back."

She stared at the waves, willing herself not to cry. It always came back to this. Guilt and promises and guilt again.

She didn't know what was worse, his angry rants or his desperate pleas for her return. She couldn't keep dragging this out. It wasn't fair...to either of them. She felt Noah's hand on her shoulder.

"You okay?" he asked.

"Yeah," she said. "Can you give me a minute?"

"Sure. I'll just walk down to check on the dogs."

"Great. Thanks."

She watched him stroll down the beach and then dialed Eddie's number.

"Eddie?" she said when he answered.

"Emily? Where are you? When are you coming home?"

"Eddie, I'm not coming back."

"Why not? I promise I'll change. I'll look harder for a job."

"It's not about the job, Eddie. It's more than that. It's the drinking too."

"Come home, Emily, and we'll work on this together. I'll go to AA."

"No, Eddie. I'm not."

"I can't believe you're doing this to me! You have to come back and help me! I can't do this without you!" Emily winced as his tone changed from pleading to angry. "You need to get back here now. Wait; are those seagulls I hear?"

"I'm not coming back, Eddie."

"It's always about you, isn't it? I want to go to school. I want to run away from home and my husband. I want," he mimicked her voice. Emily inhaled a deep breath against the pain the words were inflicting.

"Goodbye, Eddie," she whispered. She pushed the button to end the call. Damn, she thought. He had heard the seagulls. He would figure out where she was. Would he come find her? Would he make that much effort? She would have to check into an attorney soon. But, since it was Saturday, it would have to wait.

"You okay?" Noah asked after returning.

"Not really."

He nodded. "Want to go back?"

She considered returning to the bar and was tempted, but the conversation with Eddie had left her drained.

He noticed her hesitation. "Why don't you let me repay you for dinner the other night and let me cook something for you?"

"What about the others?"

"I'll send them a text," Noah said. He looked away before saying, "I suspect they're used to me disappearing by now."

"Dinner, huh?" Emily thought of someone else cooking for a change, and found the idea as appealing as Noah's company. "That sounds like a plan."

"Meet me at the houseboat in about an hour?" he asked.

"You got it."

• • • •

NOAH STIRRED THE ROUX slowly, watching the butter and flour bubble into a golden base. He added a splash of cream, then the crawfish tails, letting the scent rise. Comfort food, but elevated. Kind of like what he was hoping this night would be.

He glanced at the plate of tortillas waiting to be rolled and the pan of cheese standing by like backup dancers. "Crawfish enchiladas," he muttered to himself. "Hope she still likes these."

Sadie gave a soft woof from her corner spot, head tilted, tail tapping lazily against the cabinet.

"What? Should I have made something safe? Like spaghetti?" He looked at her. "Too late now."

The dog blinked at him, unimpressed.

He moved around the small galley kitchen, checking the oven temp, wiping down the counter for the third time. His reflection caught in the microwave door and he frowned. Shirt untucked. He tugged it straight, then ran a hand through his hair. Should he change into something else? Something that didn't say I live on a boat and only iron when there's a wedding?

Sadie made a low, bored-sounding grunt.

"I know. I'm overthinking."

He stepped back to the stove, stirring gently. The crawfish sauce had thickened just right. Not bad, considering he hadn't made this in forever. He had to do a quick internet search to look up the recipe to be sure he wasn't forgetting anything.

"You think she'll like it?" he asked.

Sadie yawned.

Noah turned off the burner and let out a long breath. His stomach tightened with something more than nerves. Hope? This was more than dinner. At least for him.

"This used to be one of her favorites," he said. "She raved about the ones she had eaten at that Lafayette restaurant one time."

He glanced around the tiny kitchen again. Candle lit. Table cleared. Napkins that didn't come from a paper towel roll. If he was going to make a fool of himself tonight, at least he'd do it with proper silverware.

He turned back to Sadie, who was watching him now, ears perked.

"You think I'm crazy, don't you?"

Sadie stood and padded over, nudging her nose against his leg.

"Yeah," he said, scratching behind her ears. "Me too. But it's a good kind of crazy."

He opened the fridge to grab a bottle of white wine. He'd been saving it for... well, he wasn't sure what. Maybe this.

# Chapter Nine

In the quiet of the cabin, Emily paced, chewing her lip. Maybe she should just cancel. It would be easier that way. No worrying about what to wear, what to say, what he might be thinking.

Should she stay? Should she go?

The temptation of the houseboat proved too much. She wanted to feel the rocking of the waves, to be near the water. She'd go, but cautiously.

She pulled on her most comfortable jeans and a Ragin' Cajuns t-shirt. A little mascara, a swipe of gloss, and she was out the door.

"Well, hello," Noah said, swinging open the gate to the houseboat and helping her aboard. "What's your poison?"

"Crown and soda."

He led her to the tiny galley. Despite the boat's age, Noah's work showed. Fresh beige paint coated the walls, and a flat-screen TV hung above a sleek sound system. Through the door at the end of the kitchen, she glimpsed a neatly made bed with a seashell-patterned coverlet. Everything was clean and precise. Military habits, probably.

A small bar lined one wall, with shelves holding a few bottles and glasses in place.

"Smells good," Emily said as the scent of seafood and spice drifted in from the kitchen.

"Seafood enchiladas." He opened the oven door to peek inside. "Not ready yet. I'm going to push off. It can finish while we enjoy the ride. Wanna take your drink outside?"

"Sure."

With Oscar and Sadie at her heels, Emily made her way to the padded lounge chairs on deck. She settled in, drink in hand, watching the shoreline disappear with the rumble of the engine.

She closed her eyes and concentrated on the rocking of the boat. She stretched out, getting comfortable. Noah turned off the engine, and it was quiet now. Only the gentle lapping of waves on the boat and soft stereo music could be heard.

"You okay with your drink?" he asked, stepping onto the deck.

"Yeah," she said, sipping slowly. Best to keep her wits. He was far too dangerous to her nervous system.

"Dinner's about ready. I just need to finish the salad. You want to eat in here or out here?" he asked, motioning to the small table.

"Out here would be perfect."

"I got it," he said when she stood. "Relax."

As Noah stepped inside Emily rested her hand on the chair's arm. The sunlight caught the glint of her wedding ring.

She turned it slowly, the way she always did when her thoughts tangled.

*What are you still holding onto?*

She wasn't sure if it was guilt, habit, or fear.

She slid the ring off and tucked it into her pocket.

She reclined back in the chair. Noah turned the music louder. This time, he'd chosen a cheesy Caribbean music channel. The song about pina coladas and getting caught in the rain made her smile. This may not be a real vacation to others, but it was for her. It was a short vacation from reality.

No Eddie. This felt heavenly. The sea air, the boat, the music. Freedom. Bliss.

• • • •

NOAH PAUSED IN THE doorway, about to speak. His breath caught as he looked at Emily. Her eyes were closed, her face relaxed. The worry lines had softened, and her lips curved into a genuine smile.

He didn't want to disturb her, but he had to put the two plates somewhere. He set them quietly on the table. Emily slowly opened her eyes.

"Looks wonderful," she said.

He'd filled the plates with cheesy seafood enchiladas, thick slices of crusty French bread, and a bright, fresh salad. He had to admit; he was proud of himself.

Emily scooted closer. Her glass was half-full, the ice melting.

"Want another drink?" he asked.

She stared at the glass for a moment. "Sure."

He stepped inside to freshen it. When he returned, she was eyeing the food.

"What's wrong?" he asked.

"Nothing. Why?"

"You haven't touched anything."

"I was waiting for you."

He smiled and took the seat across from her. "Been a while since I cooked like this."

"Oh, really?"

"Yeah. I like to cook. Not like Joey or you do. I only know a few recipes. I started cooking more after I got out of the service. Still easier to heat up a pizza or eat at Glinda's."

"You did well," she said after sampling a bite. "I may have to get the recipe."

"Sorry. Old family secret."

He wasn't about to admit he'd had to search online for the recipe. Technically, it was a family recipe now.

"Darn," she said with a smile.

He noticed the way she glanced down at her plate after meeting his eyes.

"We ate out a lot growing up. You remember? Dad was offshore a lot. Carly inherited Mom's kitchen skills. She couldn't make boxed mac and cheese without burning it. I didn't start cooking until a few years ago."

"That's a shame," Emily said.

"About my lack of interest or my mom's cooking?"

"Both," she replied, smiling.

He glanced at her glass. "Another drink?"

"Yeah, one more."

He returned with a refill, weaker this time. He'd noted her hesitation.

"I've got the estimate ready for your house," he said.

"You do? What's the damage?"

He gave her the number.

"That's not as bad as I expected."

"Like I said, mostly cosmetic. You'll be back in a few weeks. Maybe even around Christmas." He wondered if she would still be here for the holidays and hoped that she would.

She smiled, and something in him unraveled. "Really?"

"Yes."

"Thank God."

Noah began mentally rearranging his work schedule to make sure she was back in the house as soon as possible. He'd call Joey and Ryder to help one Sunday. They could work on the house, then watch the Saints.

She took a few more bites and pushed her plate away. "I'm full. It was wonderful."

"Coming from you, I'll take that as high praise."

"I guess you don't want dessert then?"

"Oh gosh, no. I don't know where I'd put it."

"Good," he chuckled. "Didn't plan that far ahead."

"You should've said something. I would've brought something."

"You wouldn't have eaten it." He teased.

"True."

"You sure you're done?" She nodded, and he stood. "I'll get these."

"Let me help."

"I got it. Sit back and enjoy."

She smiled as he disappeared into the kitchen. He rinsed the dishes and packed a plate for later.

"This music okay?" he asked when he came back.

"It's fine. It gives me a vacation vibe."

"That was the idea."

"Thank you."

"You're welcome."

He settled into the seat beside her this time. Her hand rested close to his. He wanted to reach for it, but held back. She looked relaxed, and he didn't want to ruin that.

"You look comfortable," he said.

"Actually, I am."

"That's good."

She was silent, and he was at a loss for words. She looked so peaceful sitting there. He didn't want to disturb her. Did she want him to talk? Or did she like the silence? He felt like an insecure teenager all over again. Finally, he chose to sit there with her, listening to the faint music playing and the sound of the waves.

# Chapter Ten

It was time to cook a gumbo. Joey's seafood gumbo had been great, but she was craving a chicken and sausage gumbo. She would make it from scratch, roux and all. Cooking was good for the soul, Grams always said. Emily's soul definitely needed some soothing. But first, she needed a pot to cook in.

Emily rubbed cooking oil along the inside of Grams' cast iron pot. She had cleaned out the rust, and it was time to finish "seasoning" it. The oven was preheated, and the pot wiped down with oil. All she had to do was let it sit in the oven for three hours. She would check on it periodically and put on more oil when necessary.

After sliding the pot into the oven, Emily poured a glass of wine. Not one of the best brands, but when living on a tight budget, one could not be choosy. She flinched a little at the taste, added some lemon lime soda, and then tried again. Much better.

She remembered making her first roux with her Grams. She'd been impatient with all the stirring.

...

*"That stirring is good for you, cher," Grams said after Emily complained. You ain't got nothing to do but think and stir. You know how many problems I've solved by making a roux? Most problems can be solved in the time it takes a roux if you just put your mind to it. And if you can't solve it, maybe you need to spend some time prayin' about it."*

Fourteen-year-old Emily stared down at the black cast iron pot. She had already been standing at the stove for what seemed like hours.

"Keep stirrin' cher," Grams said from the sink. "It's not ready yet."

"How do you know?" Emily asked.

"It hasn't been long enough for one thing," Grams said.

"This is taking too long," Emily said. "Why don't we use the stuff from the jar? Everyone else does."

"No roux in a jar for me cher," Grams said as she always did.

Emily grabbed the old wooden spoon and kept stirring. She was sure her arm was going to fall off before her grandma declared the roux the right color. The color of a copper penny, Grams had said.

Emily wished she'd gone fishing with Noah and Pops. She looked longingly out the window and at the blue gulf water. She'd rather be out there in the sun than cooped up in this kitchen all day stirring roux. Why did Noah have to make her mad the day before?

Talking to that other girl like that. Didn't he know she was no good for him? And when Emily had said something, Noah had gotten all mad. And Emily said she just wasn't going fishing then.

Emily heard the back door open and close. The guys must be back. She straightened her back and refused to look as they came into the kitchen.

"Hi, Emily," Noah said as he came in behind T-Pop.

"Hi Noah," Emily responded, still refusing to turn. Which was unusual. Emily and Noah had been inseparable since Emily had moved to Bon Chance.

*With her back to Grams and Pops, she missed their exchange of smiles.*

*Emily stirred the roux.*

*"Emily, why don't you go and help Noah carry in the shrimp? I'll finish up the gumbo," Grams said.*

*She shot Grams a furious glance. Grams smiled back innocently, eyes wide.*

*"Fine," Emily said. She followed Noah out the back door.*

*"Emily?" Noah said as he grabbed one end of the ice chest full of shrimp.*

*"What?" Emily asked.*

*"I'm sorry about yesterday," Noah said. "You were right. Ryder told me that Jill has been after him for weeks now. But, she didn't tell me that. I think she was trying to make him jealous."*

*"I told you so," Emily said.*

*Noah sat the ice chest down and looked at the ground. "I'm sorry, Emily. I shouldn't have bitten your head off like that."*

*Emily looked at him, his head down, his feet drawing nervous circles in the dirt, and smiled.*

*"It's okay, Noah," she said.*

*He looked up, eyes meeting hers.*

*She smiled and held her hand out. "Friends?"*

*"Always," he said.*

• • • •

EMILY SIPPED THE WINE. Maybe if she'd taken time to cook a roux, she'd have solved more problems. More time? She snorted. When?

Feeling a little cooped up, she decided to enjoy some "porch time." She grabbed a cooking magazine and the wine and headed outside. After securing Oscar to a lead, she settled into the comfortable Adirondack chair and propped her feet on the railing.

Eddie would've complained. "What are you doing?" He never actually helped with the cooking or cleaning. Even after he lost his job, he believed it was "woman's work."

One day, she'd spent the entire morning trying to bring order to the house. Eddie had woken from a stupor, stumbled to the fridge, grabbed a bottle, and minutes later passed out again. The bottle tipped and spilled beer across the floor she'd just mopped.

Emily shook her head at her own stupidity. How had she lasted that long? Too long. But not anymore.

She sipped more wine and opened the magazine, dog-earing a few recipes. After dinner, she'd take Oscar for a walk on the beach. And the wine bottle, perhaps. Let Oscar run while she planted her feet in the sand.

Her phone beeped. Great. Eddie again? His morning messages had been angry, drunk, and barely comprehensible. But this one surprised her.

**Carly:** What's up?

**Emily:** Just started seasoning a pot.

**Carly:** K. Cool. How about I come over?

**Emily**: C'mon.

**Carly**: Be there in ten. Whatcha drinkin'?

**Emily:** Wine.

**Carly:** I'll bring a bottle! Girl's night! C ya in 10.

Emily smiled and set the phone down. That was better than any text from Eddie. She stared out at the Gulf. It would be nice to have a friend to talk to. To laugh with. Soon, Carly showed up with a wine bottle under each arm.

She grinned. "I didn't ask if you wanted red or white, so I brought one of each. How's it going?"

"It's goin'," Emily said, retrieving another glass from inside the cabin and returning outside. "You?"

"Long day. I had to get my stuff from Biloxi. I'm staying with Joey for now."

"Definitely need a drink, then." Emily handed her a glass.

"You okay?" Emily asked.

"Yeah. I'll survive. I always do." Carly frowned, then shook it off. "Are you cooking something? Wish I could cook. I don't have the patience. I even tried stuff from that Homemade in Half an Hour Show. Hell, I didn't even know what she was talking about half the time. The first time I tried a recipe from that show it took me two hours! And the mess I made! Joey won't let me in his kitchen anymore."

Emily laughed, imagining Carly in a kitchen surrounded by dirty dishes and general disaster.

"Man, I can't wait for Snapper's to open. This place needs a bar." Carly said.

"Where do you even go out around here?"

"Not much of a choice here in town. We go to the Wild Wahoo sometimes. And sometimes to 31 right across the parish line. Occasionally, Joey, Noah, and I will take a night off and go to New Orleans. It's been a while since we did that, though. We are going to a Saints game soon. You should go!" Carly said.

"I might do that," Emily found herself saying.

After Carly finished her drink, Emily refilled both glasses. Carly kicked off her flip-flops and propped her glittery purple toes on the railing.

"Ahh, I gotta do this more often. So, Em," Carly said, shortening her name the way Noah had. "What's going on with you? We haven't had a chance to visit at all. How's your love life?"

Emily hesitated. "It's complicated."

"Aren't they all? I should write a book on mine. At this rate, I'm going to be that old lady with all the cats. And I don't like cats."

Emily laughed. "Might be me first. Though Oscar wouldn't like cats either."

"So glad you're back," Carly said. "Daniel talks about you a lot."

"I like Daniel. He's like another Pops."

"He's the best. Told me if I ever write a book, he'll help. He used to be a journalist."

"Have you always wanted to write?"

"Always. It's all I've ever wanted to do. I stopped for a while after graduation. Then Ryder inspired me to start again."

"Ryder?" Emily asked. She had to hear this.

"Yes. I was down in the dumps one night, and Ryder wrote a poem for me on a bar napkin. He's a poet. Inspired, I went home that night and wrote a poem in response. I've been writing ever since. It's one of the reasons I love him so much. I've told him many times that my first book will be dedicated to him."

"I hope you get published! I'd love to read it. I'm constantly on the lookout for a new book."

Carly beamed. "Cheers to that!"

They clinked glasses. The sun set pink over the blue-gray sky.

"It's a beautiful night tonight," Carly said. "Be a great night to be out on the water.

"One of these days, we'll have to get Noah to take us out on the boat. It's been a while since I've done that. We'll have Joey cook, Noah can drive the boat, and we'll drink and lie in the sun like slugs."

"Sounds good to me."

"We'll do it on a Sunday. While we lay out, the guys can watch football. We'll eat all day and watch the games."

"Let me know. It's not like my schedule is full these days."

"Hey, why don't you come work for us when we get the bar open? We'll need some help," Carly said.

"I could do that. I'll need some extra money and something to do with my time. I'd like to open my own catering company."

"That would be awesome." Carly said. "We'd be masters of our own fate with our own businesses! We should drink to that."

"I'll definitely drink to that," Emily said.

The sun was a light pink orb against a blue grey sky. Emily could see Noah and Sadie walking along the beach. He spotted the women on the porch and waved, walking over.

"What's up?" he asked from the porch steps.

"Enjoying drinks and good weather," Carly said.

"Want one?" she offered.

"Wine?" he wrinkled his nose and shook his head. "Nah."

"Go grab some beer and come join us."

He hesitated for only a moment before saying, "I think I will." Emily's pulse hitched up a notch or two at the thought of spending time with him again.

After he left, Carly smirked. "Noah's single."

Emily grinned. "Yes. He is. But I'm still married."

"Not happily, I'm guessing."

"No."

"That sucks."

"Yes. It does."

"But Noah is still single," Carly teased. "Not bad to look at, either."

Emily grinned. "Definitely not."

"Something to think about."

Noah came back with a six-pack. He took a seat on the top step.

"So, girls. What's up?"

Carly answered, "I was just getting home when I sent Em a text. She said she was here, so I thought I'd come say hi."

Noah nodded at the wine bottle between them with a grin. "And have a few."

"Of course," Carly said.

"How was today?" Noah asked Carly.

"Sucked. But at least he wasn't there. Or his woman."

"True," he turned to Emily. "And you? How was your day?"

"It was good, actually."

"That's good."

"See? We're all good. Except we're out of wine. And I don't want to mix red and white. I'm going to grab another from Glinda. I'll be right back. You two don't do anything I wouldn't do."

Noah gave Emily a wink as Carly left. "My sister is the classic social butterfly."

"And you?"

"I like quiet. A cold beer with good friends. Not a fan of bars."

They drank in silence for a beat.

"I cleaned shrimp and crab this afternoon. One of my customers gave me some. Too much for me. Want some?"

"Sure. We'll cook."

"Cook?" Carly asked, walking up with a bottle of wine under one arm.

"Yeah, we have some shrimp and crabs," Noah said.

"Why don't we cook them up tonight?" Carly suggested.

"We?" Noah asked, raising a dark eyebrow at his sister.

"Okay, I'll provide moral support. And drinks," Carly smiled. "I'll call Joey; we'll make a night of it. And he can cook too."

She picked up the phone to call Joey. After a quick conversation, hung up. "He's coming. I'm gonna grab some beer from the store. I'll meet y'all back over here. You want wine or beer?"

"Whatever you bring is fine," Emily said.

"Cool," Carly said. She slipped on flip-flops and was gone.

"Any idea what you want to cook?" Noah asked.

"Shrimp and crab, obviously."

Noah grinned, "Obviously. How about grilling the shrimp? There's a built-in pit right over there. Joey does this thing where he wraps the shrimp in bacon with some pepper jack cheese. It's fantastic. And since we're grilling, how about burgers and hot dogs?"

"That sounds awesome."

"Well, I'll wait for him, and he and I will run to the store to pick up whatever else we need. What about the crab? Any ideas?"

"How about a crab dip? We'll keep it simple."

"Perfect," he said. "Make a list and we'll pick it up."

"Sounds good."

Carly came back with Ryder in tow.

"I found a straggler," Carly said.

Ryder grinned. "I never turn down a meal from a pretty female. It's a rule."

Noah coughed, "You would if you'd eaten Carly's cooking."

"Yeah, but Carly's not cooking. I know better than that."

Carly grinned devilishly. "So, Emily, tell Ryder what you're doing."

"What do you mean?"

"When I sent you that text earlier. What did you say you were doing?"

"Seasoning my pot?" Emily asked.

"Yes, Ryder. Emily is seasoning her pot today."

Here we go, Emily thought.

"Is that right?" Ryder asked her, "I bet I can help with that. I'm hot enough to season any pot."

Emily shook her head, "Ryder, you're about to talk yourself out of a free meal."

Ryder took his black cowboy hat off and put it on Emily's head. "Ah, but you see, I bet I can talk myself right back into it."

• • • •

THE GUYS HAD RETURNED from the store and were crowded around the BBQ pit, drinking beer and talking football. Carly had poured more drinks, and she and Emily were sitting around the fire pit. Emily had fixed the crab dip, and it was bubbling in the oven along with the seasoning pot.

Emily had sent Glinda a text, and she was on her way with Daniel.

It was becoming a party.

Emily sipped silently, taking it all in. She kept one eye on Oscar who, unbelievably, was actually behaving himself. Sadie was a good influence. She kept him exercised and in check.

Carly got up to go turn the radio on in Joey's Jeep. "What are we in the mood for tonight, guys?"

"Anything but country," Noah said.

"How about some 80s?" Carly asked.

"Fine. Stick to rock though. No Belinda Carlisle for me. No cheese, please," Noah said, and Joey nodded.

Carly adjusted the radio to an 80s station and soft music drifted over to the small circle of chairs around the fire pit. Later, they would light a fire, Noah had promised, as he had placed some firewood down earlier.

Carly and Emily propped their feet up on the rock-edged fire pit and sipped their drinks. They watched as Noah and Ryder began setting up chairs and tables. "Should we help?" Emily asked.

"Nah. They got that," Carly said. "It's our job to sit here and relax."

"I can handle that."

Glinda and Daniel walked up. Glinda with a bowl and Daniel had a bag of French bread.

"Where should we put this, pretty ladies?" Daniel asked.

Carly pointed to the group of guys. "I think they're putting all the food over there."

"Have a seat, Glinda, and I'll take this over there," Daniel said.

Glinda joined Carly and Emily. "Want a drink?" Carly asked.

"I'll take a glass of wine. But, I'll get it, don't get up."

Ryder walked over to them, bowl in hand. He slid into the seat with Emily, sitting on her lap. Emily looked at Carly, who rolled her eyes.

"Look what I got, Miss Emily. Some potato salad."

Emily shook her head, but laughed at the glint in his eyes. "No."

"Sure?" he asked, grinning.

"Positive."

He sighed dramatically and unfolded his tall body from the seat. He sat on the arm of Glinda's seat, "What about you, Ms. Glinda?"

Glinda slapped him on the arm. "If I were about twenty years younger, you'd be in trouble, young man. I'd wear you out! Now, go on and either eat that potato salad or put it up. There will be no wasting food."

"Yes, ma'am," he said, and tipped his hat at the women before rejoining the guys.

Emily checked the time on her phone. It was time to check the crab dip and put another coat of oil on the pot.

"I'll be right back," she told Glinda and Carly.

Emily pulled the hot pot out of the stove and put it safely on a folded dish towel. She coated a big wad of paper towels with cooking oil.

She looked out the window as she worked. Glinda and Carly were visiting. Glinda was laughing at something Carly was saying. The guys were still standing around the BBQ pit. When her eyes caught Noah's and he smiled, her stomach did crazy flip-flops. She held the gaze, not looking down for once. He winked, and his lips curved in a sultry smile.

She smiled back. Life was so much better with these people in it. They were her "seasoning." They added spice, comfort, and laughter to her life. Qualities that her life had been missing until now.

She finished up in the kitchen and went outside.

"Emily," Noah called as she walked down the steps. "Come, try this shrimp."

Noah held out a bacon-wrapped shrimp as she walked up. She hesitated for a moment, when he held it up to her lips. He fed her the shrimp and her eyes closed in rapture. The smoky bacon, the spicy cheese, the salty shrimp was a little bite of heaven. She opened her eyes to see Noah watching as she licked her lips. Emily had to force herself to pull her gaze away.

"That is incredible," Emily said to Joey.

"Thanks," Joey said, smiling.

"Emily!" Carly called and jogged up, Emily's phone in her hand. "Your phone is going off."

Emily froze. It had to be Eddie. When she reached out to grab the phone, Carly's hand slipped, accidentally swiping to answer the phone.

"Emily!" Eddie was in a rage again. His voice was loud enough to be heard by everyone around her.

"Who's that?" Ryder asked, looking at Carly.

"Who is that?" Eddie yelled. "Are you with a man?"

Emily scrambled to hang up the phone, her hands shaking.

"You slut!" Eddie yelled before she could end the call.

Emily dropped the phone and bent down to pick it up, but Ryder beat her to it.

"What did you just say?" He asked into the phone. He paused for a moment and said, "Oh? Is that right?"

Emily's stomach knotted up as she listened to the rest of the conversation.

"Well, I'll tell you what. We don't talk to women like that."

Emily watched as Ryder's eyes flashed, all hints of humor gone. "My name is Ryder. R-y-d-e-r. And I'm right here in Bon Chance, Louisiana. You come right on down. I'll be glad to continue this conversation." He hung up the phone and handed it to Emily.

Emily's stomach rolled. She was speechless. She sensed Noah's presence beside her. His hand cradled her elbow.

"C'mon, Em. Let's take a walk. Let's go get some air."

Emily let Noah lead her away. She heard the group talking as she left.

"Oh my God," said Carly. "I didn't mean to answer the phone."

"Poor girl," said Joey.

Their pity and concern made Emily feel worse.

Noah led her down the beach, out of sight and hearing from the group.

"Lean over," he said. "Put your hands on your knees."

She looked at him questioningly.

"Trust me," he said.

She did as instructed.

"Now. Close your eyes. Breathe in. Breathe out," he said. "Say it to yourself as you do it. Breathe in. Breathe out."

He crouched down beside her and placed a hand on her shoulder.

"Breathe in. Breathe out."

It worked. Slowly, Emily's hand stopped trembling. She opened her eyes after her breathing finally regulated.

"Now, sit down," he said, motioning her over to a concrete picnic table.

Emily was glad to do it. Her legs still trembled. Noah sat down beside her. He didn't touch her, though. He let her keep some distance.

Emily put her elbows on her knees and her face in her hands. She stared at the sand. At her feet. At anything but Noah.

"Why?" she asked.

Noah said nothing. Didn't ask "why what?"

"I was just standing there in the house. I was looking at all of you guys. And I was happy. For the first time in months. I was happy. I forgot what happiness even felt like."

She lifted her face to look at him.

"How sad is that? How sad is it that someone forgets what happy is? Emily's eyes filled with tears. "He ruined it. He ruined my perfectly happy day. He humiliated me. I am so embarrassed."

"Why, Emily?" he asked.

"Why?"

"Why are you embarrassed? You did nothing wrong."

"But."

"But, nothing. That's his bad behavior. That has nothing to do with you," Noah said. "You can't control that."

"But, it's my fault."

"No, Emily. It's not. As far as I can tell, you did absolutely the right thing by coming home. You don't deserve to be treated like that."

She gave him a shaky smile. "You are right."

"Yes. I am," he smiled back, "You okay?"

"I will be," she said.

"Yes. You will." he reached out and pulled her close. Emily rested her head on his shoulder for a second and closed her eyes. She took a deep breath, knowing that he was right. She would be okay.

· · · ·

THE REST OF THE GROUP were gathered around the fire pit when they returned.

Joey looked up to see Noah and Emily walking up. "Hey, y'all! We were waiting for you guys to eat. The food's all ready."

"The crab dip!" Emily exclaimed. She had forgotten about it.

"I got it, cher," Glinda said.

"And I took care of your pot," Ryder grinned. "Looks to me like it needs some more seasoning. It's not hot enough. It needs some spice."

Emily smiled. "My pot is fine." Seasoned almost perfectly, she thought as she looked up at Noah. Ryder was right. It could use some more spice. And Noah was the one to add it.

After they finished eating, Joey asked, "S'mores anyone?"

Glinda yawned. "I'll pass, but thank you. I think I'll be heading back up to the house."

Daniel nodded as well.

"I'd love some s'mores," Emily said after Daniel and Glinda had said their goodbyes.

She hadn't had s'mores since she was a kid and had gone camping with her grandparents. They had stayed up making wishes on falling stars and stuffing themselves with chocolate and marshmallows. She remembered one particular wish when she was sixteen. She had wished that Noah Devereaux would kiss her. She smiled. She looked up at the stars and again wished that Noah Devereaux would kiss her. Damn the consequences. It was time she had something good in her life.

Interrupting her thoughts, Joey tossed her the bag of marshmallows. Noah handed her a weathered stick with a point whittled at the end. She scooted closer to the fire so she could reach. Noah reached for the bag and soon all of them were roasting their marshmallows in relative silence.

"Damn it!" Carly said, shaking out the burning mass on the end of the stick.

"Seriously, Carly?" Joey said, "How do you mess up s'mores?"

He grabbed the stick. "Here, let me do it."

She snatched it back. "I can do it."

Emily glanced at Noah, who only shook his head and sipped his beer. Oscar and Sadie, done with their beach inspection and finding all satisfactory, came back to the fire and settled in between Noah and Emily. Oscar sniffed at the stick with the marshmallow on it, but, finding it lacking, laid his head down.

Carly and Joey finished their argument and settled back onto their seats. Carly stubbornly ate the burnt s'more while Joey laughed at her.

"I told you to let me do it," he said.

She glared at him and finished the s'more. She licked the gooey marshmallow off her fingers, then looked at the group. "So, how bout we all do a bar crawl? What do you think?"

Noah said, "Why do we have to do anything? Let's just relax for now."

"Okay." Carly said. "But, soon. We need to take Emily out and show her the sights."

"We will," promised Noah.

The rest of the night passed uneventfully. Ryder left early. It was ladies' night at 31. And they had a band. So, that just left the four of them. Soon, lulled by the fire, the food, and the company, Emily stifled a yawn.

"It is getting late," Noah said. "I think I'm about ready to turn in myself. Joey? You mind helping me clean up?"

The four of them made quick work of the mess, and soon Carly and Joey were hugging Emily bye and heading home. Noah walked Emily up the stairs to her door. Stopping in front of the door, Emily stopped and looked up at the stars. She wished Noah Devereaux would kiss her.

"Noah?" Emily said. "Thank you."

"You're very welcome."

Emily looked up into his eyes. Emily saw his eyes darken in the pale light of the moon. He leaned in. She was going to get her wish.

*Slut!* Echoed through her mind.

Involuntarily, Emily flinched and turned away. Noah took a step back. She could see his confusion.

"Noah, Noah. I'm sorry."

A sad smile flickered across his lips. "It's okay, Emily. Good night."

Emily watched as he whistled for Sadie and walked away.

• • • •

THE SHOP WASN'T MUCH. An old weathered shed next door to the bait shop that was soon to be Snapper's. The tin roof still rattled when the wind kicked up, but inside, it was steady. Solid. It smelled like cedar shavings, old coffee, and wood stain.

Noah flipped on the light. It buzzed before flooding the space with soft gold, catching on the edges of sawdust and half-finished projects. The cypress table he'd been working on stood in the center.

He picked up the sanding block and worked it over the grain, slow and sure. The wood had come from an old porch out in Breaux Bridge. He remembered the day he picked it up. It was a humid summer afternoon, typical for a Louisiana summer day. On the drive back, windows down and radio low, he'd thought of her.

Emily.

He hadn't seen her in years, but he'd known she was living in Lafayette. Not far, really. Close enough. He remembered wondering what she might be doing. Had she finished college? Taken a job in a big hotel? Was she happy?

Only now, he knew she hadn't been.

His hand paused. He stared at the swirling pattern in the wood, then picked the sander back up and pushed harder.

He should've gone to see her. Should've followed that instinct.

But what would he have found?

Not the Emily he'd imagined that day. Not the girl with laughter in her eyes and music in her step. She'd been hurting. Stuck. And he hadn't known.

That part sat heavy in his chest.

Noah grabbed the chisel and mallet and started carving a scroll into the table's edge. It reminded him of the old rocking chair she used to love at her grandmother's place, the one she'd curl into with a dog-eared paperback.

She'd always been like that. Soft places and sharp edges. A quiet kind of magic.

The wood curled away in perfect spirals. It helped ease his nerves. Woodworking always did.

But then that memory, Eddie's voice on the phone, venom laced into every syllable. Emily's face crumpling, the flinch she couldn't hide. The apology she never should've had to give.

His jaw tightened. His grip on the chisel did too.

There was a moment where he imagined driving to Lafayette. No warning. No words. Just showing up at Eddie's door and seeing what kind of man inflicted harm on someone like her. He still had connections in the military and law enforcement. It wouldn't be hard to find the address.

But he didn't need to. Not really.

Because Emily was here now. With him. With all of them. She was healing. Laughing again.

He wiped the sweat from his brow and stepped back from the table.

It wasn't finished. But it was strong. Seasoned. Full of quiet beauty and second chances.

Kinda like her.

He brushed the curls of wood off the bench, then, on a whim, reached for his pencil. On the underside of the table, small and out of sight, he scribbled one word:

*Emily.*

He smiled to himself and went back to work.

# Chapter Eleven

Emily curled up on the worn sofa, her feet tucked underneath. Her mom's faded blanket was wrapped around her legs. She had a cup of mint tea in one hand and a paperback novel in the other. The house was quiet after everyone had gone home and Emily grabbed a book, hoping it would take her mind off Noah and that almost kiss.

A voracious reader in high school, she had been the librarians' greatest love and greatest challenge. She rarely met a book she didn't like. Growing up poor, she'd often escaped in her dreams to faraway lands, places filled with sights and sounds beyond her reach. In books, she got to escape the shyness, and self-consciousness. She was the confident, brave heroines in the books. She was Scarlett O'Hara, Jo March, or Cherry Valance. The irony of the situation with Noah tonight was not lost on her.

Unfortunately, the book she picked tonight was hitting too close to home. The author's quest mirrored hers in such a way it made her uncomfortable. The author's depression hit too close to home. She grabbed another book from the pile. She needed a good murder mystery, but there was none. Murder, clues, arrest. Cut and dried. No shades of gray for her.

Oscar stirred on the floor, content after a long walk, rather run, on the beach with Sadie. She knew he had to be happier here. Not stuck in some boring back yard for hours while she worked.

Was she happy? She thought about it for a second. Not really happy as much as content. Peaceful. Not happy yet, but she'd take it. For now, anyway.

She sipped her tea and picked up the next book, a historical romance set in New Orleans. The cover featured a busty brunette in a billowing dress clinging to a roguish-looking man, the wrought-iron balconies of the French Quarter glinting behind them. When she was in the mood to read romance, those were her favorites. She loved the drama, the danger, the secrets whispered through lace fans and gaslit alleyways. If time travel was real, she'd visit that era in a heartbeat. Of course, after two hours of corsets, cobblestones, and no air conditioning, she'd probably tap out and head straight back to modern comforts.

Three chapters into the book, she slammed it shut with a frustrated sigh. She found herself resenting the main character. Envying her for having this fine, dark-headed man pursue her. That didn't happen in real life. In real-life, there weren't any fairy-tale happy endings.

The phone rang, shattering the silence. She picked it up from off the blanket. It was Eddie. Again.

"Slut." The word flashed on the phone screen. A text she had no choice but to see.

She resisted the urge to throw the phone, pocketing it instead. She slipped shoes on and headed out the door. Eager to escape, running away from Eddie. Again.

"Slut," echoed in her head as she dropped and sat on the sand, wrapping her arms around her knees.

There were no screeching birds tonight. The waves made a soft splash against the sand as if they knew it was night and it was time for quiet. Occasionally, a loud burst of laughter from customers of the inn would break through. She supposed she could have gone in there, been around people. But she wanted to be alone, needed to be alone.

The sea breeze blew a lock of hair across her face that she tucked behind an ear. She had always wanted to go to the beach with Eddie, but there had never been time when he was working. He had been driven then, ready to climb the ladder. Working to make a name for himself. There was never time to get away. Then, after that non-promotion, she hadn't been able to tear him away from a new mistress, the slender brown bottle that made him forget he had problems.

Then, there wasn't any money. Broke and exhausted, she hadn't even thought of a vacation. Eddie was the last person she would've wanted to vacation with. Who wanted to spend a vacation babysitting a drunk?

"Slut," echoed in her mind again. She felt a tear well up. Then another. Then another. She didn't resist this time. She let them fall.

· · · ·

NOAH WAS STANDING ON the deck of the houseboat, nursing a beer and lost in thought. He had just come home from the shop and he was restless. His arms rested on the rails. He watched as the sweat from the bottle dripped down to the inky water below. He thought of Emily. The hurt in her brown eyes he saw too often. How he loved it when he could get her to drop that guard and laugh. That woman had little to smile about. He could tell. It was written all over her face, especially in her eyes. He could definitely relate. He'd been there himself.

For years, after Iraq, after Benjamin's death, he had that same haunted look. And that same empty feeling inside.

There was movement on the beach. A solitary figure. That was unusual. Usually, it was couples strolling along the beach, stealing kisses in the moonlight. Driving Noah into his house, cursing for interrupting his evening. He had no desire to be a voyeur.

He recognized Emily in the pale moonlight. She sank down onto the sand, head lowered, body curled up. She looked like she had lost a best friend.

Should he go to her? Ask her if she was okay? Would she think it was an intrusion? He hesitated.

Then, she brushed something off her cheeks. She was crying. And his mind was made up.

· · · ·

EMILY HEARD THE SLOW scrunch of footsteps approaching on the sand. She sniffed and brushed away the tears with a frustrated hand. Aggravated, someone was intruding. When she saw Noah, her breath caught. Part of her wanted to lean into him. Part of her wasn't sure she should.

He plopped down on the sand beside her silently and pulled her close to his side. She rested her head on his shoulder, accepting the comfort he was offering. She closed her eyes and sighed.

"You okay?" he asked finally.

"I will be," she said. And she would be. Eventually.

"Yes, you will be." He tightened his hold on her slightly. He smelled good. Like salty sea air. He was shoeless; the ends of his jeans were slightly tattered. He looked like the stereotypical beach bum with his shaggy hair. A light beard shadowed the bottom half of his face. So inconsistent with the military man he must have been a few years ago.

She should scoot away, but didn't want to. She wanted to stay exactly where she was. Tucked right next to him, feeling his warmth. Besides, sometimes a girl simply wanted a shoulder to lean on. And what a nice shoulder it was. It was solid. Dependable. She knew she shouldn't be thinking like that. It was dangerous. But she didn't care. At that moment, there was no way she was going to move her head from his shoulder. She had felt all alone for too long.

Another stray tear escaped, and she brushed it away. Noah seemed to respect her need for silence. He ran a hand slowly up and down her upper arm, as if trying to keep her warm. It was hard to thaw someone from the inside out, though. Especially when the chill had nothing to do with the cool night air.

Emily shivered a little, and Noah hugged her a little closer.

"Thank you," she finally said.

"You're welcome."

"I guess I needed this." her voice was still shaky, and it was irritating.

"You probably did."

"I haven't really cried in months until now. Seemed like a waste of time."

"There's nothing wrong with it."

"I know." She shot him a sideways glance. "How did you know I was here, by the way?"

He pointed to the lights on the boat. "I was having a drink on the deck. I saw you."

"Oh."

He nodded toward the boat. "You want to come join me? Looks like you could use a drink."

She was tempted, but she shook her head. "I think I'll pass this time. I think I'd just like to go back to my place. Get some sleep."

"I understand. Let me walk you home, then."

"You don't have to do that. It's right there."

"Yeah, I know, but it makes me feel like a gentleman. I don't get to do that too much."

She gave a little half chuckle, voicing her disbelief. "I bet."

"I swear!" he said, holding a hand out to help her up. "This place is not exactly swarming with beautiful, single women."

"You're something else, you know that Noah?" she said, smiling. She wondered if that was a compliment, as she was not a single woman. Yet.

"That's what you keep telling me."

"Maybe cause it's the truth."

He walked with her in silence, stopping in front of her door. "Good night, Emily."

"Night, Noah."

She stared up at him, nervously she grabbed for her hair to cover the scar on her cheek from that car accident so many years ago. Noah gently grabbed her hand.

"Emily, we all have scars. With some of us, you just can't see them."

He stared at her for a moment; she knew he wanted to kiss her. He leaned in close. And kissed her cheek. It was a sweet gesture that left her frustrated.

"Get some sleep. Things will look so much better in the morning,"

He turned and left. Leaving her alone. She watched him cross the street to the houseboat, brown hair blowing in the breeze. Sleep no longer seemed appealing.

• • • •

NOAH RESUMED HIS SPOT on the deck of the boat. He sipped a beer, feet propped up on the railing. Rock music drifted through the speakers installed recently. He kept the music on most nights because music gave his mind something to hold on to. After Iraq, after Benjamin, he'd learned that stillness was a breeding ground for memories. Rock helped. The kind with grit and volume. Something that shook loose the ghosts and drowned out the voices of the past.

Tonight, it wasn't just the past tugging at him. It was Emily. She kept slipping into his thoughts. Those guarded brown eyes, that quiet strength. He saw something familiar in her. That look of someone who knew what it was to lose something and carry on anyway.

Noah remembered the nights he had spent on the beach when he'd returned. When he'd watched the waves and thought of the past. Now he spent his time on the deck. He'd had his own nights like hers. Still had them occasionally. Certain dates, certain moments, sent him back to this beach. Carly and Joey always left him alone. He preferred it that way. Carly and Joey would hang out together. Joey would be there for Carly as he always had been. And Noah, the oldest, would take care of himself.

He heard footsteps on the pier. It was Joey. Too heavy for Carly. And no flip-flop sound. That woman wore sandals almost 365 days a year. He had long ago grown tired of fussing.

Joey rounded the corner. "Hey man. Saw your light on. Thought I'd swing by."

"Cool. Grab a beer." Noah settled on to one of the chairs on the deck.

Joey ducked into the open door and, after snagging the beer, sat in the chair beside him. "So, what's been going on?"

"Not much," Noah said.

Joey rubbed the back of his neck. "Man... when Carly answered Emily's phone." He shook his head. "Made my stomach turn. You know this wasn't the first time." He paused. "And Carly? I don't think she's stopped feeling guilty since. I wish we would have known."

"Yeah." Noah tightened his grip on his glass. He didn't know what to say. Hell, he was still trying to make sense of it himself. The anger, the way Emily's face had crumpled. It all twisted together. So, he changed the subject. "What's Carly up to tonight? She at home?"

"Yeah. She's going through old pictures of her and her ex. I can hear her crying in the room. I know she'd be pissed if I went in there."

Noah wanted to ask Joey when he was finally going to man up and tell Carly how he felt, but had long ago told himself to stay out of it. Hopefully, things would all work out in the end. At least that's what he kept telling himself. After years of Joey pining after Carly, he wasn't so sure. Carly, for all her people smarts, was blind when it came to herself. She was crazy about Joey, and Joey was crazy about her. It made Noah crazy to watch them. He just shook his head.

They sipped their drinks in silence for a while. Joey stretched his legs out and propped them on the railing.

"Oh, I got the rooms booked for that Saints game," Joey said.

"Cool. I can't wait. I need to get away. Carly ever decide if she was going or not?"

"You know how she is. She'll make up her mind at the last minute."

"She's going. Carly miss a trip to New Orleans?" Noah said.

"I know. Maybe you can ask Emily?"

"Maybe so," Noah replied.

Joey took another sip of beer and was silent. Joey wanted Carly. But Joey wouldn't do anything about it. The man was terrified. Terrified it would work out and things would be great. Terrified it would work out and change things. Noah did not envy him one bit.

They sat in silence for a while. Drinking and looking out at the water. Later, Joey's phone beeped.

"That's Carly." Joey unfolded himself from the deck chair. "I'm heading home. Thanks for the beer."

"No prob man. Anytime."

Noah watched Joey as he walked down the dock. His head was slightly lowered and the familiar bounce in his step was missing. Something was eventually going to have to change in that situation. Noah downed the rest of his drink and whistled for Sadie. He was exhausted.

# Chapter Twelve

The morning sun warmed the wide porch of the Redbird Inn, filtering through the trees. A breeze rolled in from the gulf, carrying the scent of saltwater and petunias. Emily sat in one of the old wicker rockers, hands wrapped around a warm mug of tea.

Glinda settled into the chair beside her, her own mug resting on the armrest, steam curling up in the cool air like a lazy dancer.

For a while, they said nothing. The quiet between them wasn't awkward. It was the kind of silence that existed only between people who understood each other without needing to fill space.

Finally, Emily broke it.

"I changed my number this morning."

Glinda glanced over, one brow rising slightly. "You did?"

Emily nodded. "Sent him a message first. Told him if he needed to contact me again, he could do it through an attorney."

She took a sip of her tea. Her hands trembled just a little.

"But, I don't have an attorney," she added, almost like an afterthought.

Glinda's voice was soft. "That's a hell of a first step, *cher.* Brave."

"It didn't feel brave," Emily said. "It felt... overdue. Like finally cutting a cord that's been strangling me for years."

Glinda reached over and gave her hand a squeeze. "Still brave. Even overdue things can scare the hell out of us."

Footsteps thudded up the steps from the side yard. Daniel appeared, holding a carton of fresh eggs in one hand.

"Mornin', ladies," he said, setting the eggs on the little table between them. "Thought y'all could use these. Got 'em from Leon's coop this morning. Those hens are laying like their lives depend on it."

"You're wonderful," Glinda said, already reaching for the carton. "I'll whip us up some omelettes in the morning."

Daniel looked between them and picked up on the mood. "Everything okay?"

"We were just talking attorneys," Glinda said with a smile. "Seems we need one."

Emily sat up a little straighter. "I told Eddie to go through a lawyer from now on. But I... I don't have one yet."

Daniel scratched his jaw. "I might know someone. Pete Jagneaux. Has a little practice up in Houma. Mostly does family stuff. Solid guy. Owes me a favor, actually."

"You think he'd take me on?" Emily asked, uncertain.

Daniel pulled out his phone and gave her a wink. "Let me call him. If he says no, I'll twist his arm a little. He'll at least meet with you."

As he stepped away to make the call, Glinda leaned in, voice low. "See there? You don't have to figure it all out alone. One step at a time."

Emily looked out over the porch railing. The trees swayed gently, and somewhere in the distance, she heard the low hum of a boat heading out.

Maybe she didn't know everything yet. But for the first time in a long time, she had a direction.

And that felt like something.

• • • •

EMILY'S PHONE BUZZED just after she rinsed her teacup and set it in the drying rack. She glanced around the kitchen. Everything was too neat, too tidy, and way too quiet. The laundry was done. The dishes were put away, and she was too restless to sit with a book, though she'd tried twice already. She paced to the window, arms crossed, and watched the breeze rustle the garden outside. Morning was slipping toward noon, and she still didn't know what to do with the rest of the day. That aimless feeling had started to creep in again, the kind that made her skin itch.

Her phone lit up on the counter.

**Carly:** Hey. I'm heading over to Snapper's in a bit. Wanna come help? I need a distraction. And maybe some company.

Emily stared at the message for a moment, thumb hovering. She could say no. She had every excuse. But the truth was, she needed a distraction too. Something that didn't involve wondering what the hell she was going to say to a divorce attorney.

**Emily:** Same. Lawyer tomorrow. I'll be there in twenty.

Snapper's still smelled like drywall and dust, but progress was visible. New bar stools were stacked neatly by the bar. Carly was crouched by a box of bar glasses, wiping her face with the hem of her t-shirt.

Emily let herself in. "How can I help?"

Carly looked up, her face pink from effort. "Did you bring caffeine and a magic wand?."

Emily held up two iced coffees. "Best I could do."

Carly laughed and took one. "You're a damn lifesaver."

They got to work in comfortable silence. Emily sorted glassware behind the bar while Carly dug through boxes of supplies, muttering about needing a better inventory system.

"Why are there three cases of martini glasses?" Carly asked, popping open another box.

"No clue. Maybe you were feeling optimistic."

Carly rolled her eyes, reaching into the box just as the bottom gave way with a dramatic thunk. A cascade of assorted contents tumbled out, but it was the forgotten bottle of grenadine inside that really made an impression. It bounced once... and then exploded in a sticky red splash across both of them.

"Oh no," Emily gasped.

Carly froze, dripping crimson syrup down her front. "Well. That's one way to christen the bar."

Emily blinked, then started laughing. Carly joined in, shaking her hands out like a cat who'd stepped in something offensive.

"Remind me to never ask you for help again," Carly teased.

"You're the one who dropped it."

They were still laughing as they grabbed towels and started mopping themselves off, the tension of the last few days finally cracking just a little at the edges.

"God," Carly said, breathless. "I think I needed that."

Emily nodded, her smile fading just a little. "Me too."

They paused to drink some water, sitting on upturned crates like queens on temporary thrones.

Carly broke the quiet as she wiped at her syrup-streaked shirt. "You'd think after five years with A.J., I'd be better at cleaning up messes."

Emily shot her a look. "Emotional or literal?"

"Both," Carly muttered, managing a crooked smile.

"Sometimes the mess teaches you more than the easy parts," Emily said quietly.

Carly blinked. "You been reading fortune cookies again?"

"Nope. Just living one."

That got a smile. Carly nudged her knee. "So. You see the attorney tomorrow?"

Emily nodded. "I do."

"You okay?"

"No. But I'm going anyway."

Carly gave her a solemn nod. "Damn right you are."

They clinked their plastic bottles together like they were toasting something sacred.

"New starts," Carly said.

"Clean slates," Emily replied.

"Or at least disinfected ones," Carly added, gesturing to the bar.

They got back to work. Not to fix everything, but enough to feel like they were.

• • • •

THE SAW WHINED AS NOAH fed the board through. But his head wasn't in it. He caught himself pressing unevenly and eased back before the blade could splinter the edge. He sighed and shut the machine off, rubbing the back of his neck.

Sadie lifted her head from where she was curled up under the bench.

He was making a shelf for Carly. Nothing fancy, but it might as well have been a cathedral with the way he was struggling to concentrate.

Outside, a truck door slammed.

Joey stepped into the workshop holding two gas station coffees and a paper sack that smelled vaguely of fried something. "Figured you could use a break."

Noah accepted the cup, still annoyed with the board. "Appreciate it. You on grocery duty?"

"Ran to Prejean's. Carly's trying to make fancy sandwiches for dinner and forgot the bread." Joey held up the sack. "Also got boudin balls. You're welcome."

Noah smirked. "She ever gonna learn to cook?"

"She says boiling water is a talent, not a guarantee."

They leaned against the worktable, sipping coffee.

"You saw her today?" Joey asked.

Noah didn't have to ask who "her" was. "No."

"Carly said she stopped by Snapper's. Helped clean up. Said she looked better. Not fine, but... not like yesterday."

Noah nodded slowly.

"You going over there tonight?"

"Probably not."

Joey let the silence stretch before saying, "She's tougher than I gave her credit for."

"Yeah. She is." Noah exhaled. "I just don't want to push her into anything before she's ready."

"She's not made of glass, man. Just dented up a little."

Noah gave him a look. "We all are."

Joey snorted. "Fair point."

Noah laughed, a low rasp in his throat. "Drop a plate by if Carly gives up and you end up cooking."

"Will do."

As Joey turned to leave, he said, "Just... don't disappear on her, Noah. Even if she says she needs space."

Noah didn't answer right away. He just looked down at the shelf. "I'm here. She knows that."

Sadie thumped her tail.

# Chapter Thirteen

"Ms. Breaux, Mr. Jagneaux will see you now."

Emily stood on legs that felt like they might give out at any second. She smoothed her shirt, gave the receptionist a grateful nod, and followed her into a small office that had a faint scent of lemon oil and old books.

The man behind the desk looked up from a legal pad, glasses sliding halfway down his nose. He wore a polo shirt and the kind of deeply weathered expression only years of gulf coast sun could give you.

"You're Emily?" he asked, voice gravelly but kind.

"Yes, sir. Thank you for seeing me on short notice."

"Well, the fish weren't biting this morning, so you lucked out." He gestured to the seat across from him. "What can I help you with?"

"I need a divorce," she said, and surprised herself by how steady it came out.

He nodded. "All right. We'll get started. And just so I have it right. What name are you filing under?"

"Breaux." she said. "But, I want to change my name back to my maiden name, Thibodeaux."

He gave her a small smile. "Understood."

As they spoke, Emily explained the basics—no shared property, no children, and that she wanted as little contact as possible.

"I'd like all future contact to go through you. I've changed my phone number already. I don't want him to reach me at all. Not by phone, by email, by anything."

His pen paused. "Has he ever threatened you?"

"Not physically. Not directly," she said. "But... he's controlling. And he gets angry fast. A couple of nights ago, he screamed at me over the phone. In front of people. Called me names." Her cheeks flushed.

Mr. Jagneaux nodded, jotting something down. "You want to include a no-contact clause in the divorce decree. I can also file for a temporary protective order if needed. Sometimes that cools the tempers."

She hesitated. "Let's see how he reacts first."

"Fair enough. But if he does reach out, or shows up, you call me. Or the sheriff if necessary. Don't wait."

Emily nodded, pressing her hands together to stop their trembling.

After agreeing to his terms and signing the necessary paperwork, she stepped back out into the bright afternoon sun. The air smelled like salt and hibiscus. Her phone felt strange in her pocket, like it belonged to a different version of herself. She looked up at the sky, whispering a silent prayer that Eddie would sign the papers and let her go.

But deep down, she knew better.

• • • •

EMILY GRABBED A PAIL and a small assortment of cleaning supplies and climbed the steps of her grandparents' house. Now her house. She'd started the process of cleaning Eddie out of her life. Now it was time to tackle the rest.

The hole in the roof had left more than water stains. Dampness clung to the walls, and the faint odor of mildew hit her before she even reached the kitchen.

Noah would help with the windows. They'd already planned a run to New Orleans for supplies. Soon, she'd be picking out paint colors, choosing curtains, laying out rugs. Not to please anyone else, but for herself. For the first time in a long time, she got to decide.

She threw open the windows. The gulf breeze rolled in, tangled her hair, and chased the stale air out. Dust motes danced in the shafts of morning light. The place creaked like an old ship, settling around her as if waking up after a long sleep.

She started with the cabinets. Bleach met salt in the back of her throat as she scrubbed. Her hands ached, her back protested, but she didn't stop.

As she scrubbed, her thoughts wandered. She thought of Noah. That spark. She'd felt that for Eddie once. That was a long time ago. It seemed like a different lifetime. They had been so in love. The world melted away when she had been in his arms. It was the two of them against the world. Like the montage of images and music in a bad soap opera, the memories flashed through her mind.

That first kiss, full of promises they'd both believed. Their wedding day. The day he was fired. The long descent into alcoholism that followed.

She had fought to hold it all together, patching up holes, soothing bruises, literal and otherwise. And still, it had crumbled.

She stood in the kitchen, eyes stinging, fists clenched. There was nothing soft left in her for him.

Tears welled up and she angrily pushed them away with a wet hand. She wouldn't shed one more tear for Eddie. A new life lay ahead, and she was free. She would create a very different life, but a new life. HER life. And she'd be damned if she'd let Eddie ruin it.

• • • •

"EMILY?" HE STEPPED inside, toolbox in hand. "I saw your car out front. Figured I'd check if you needed anything."

His voice caught when he saw her.

She stood at the counter, a damp rag dangling from one hand. Her shoulders were slumped, and tears streamed down her face. When she looked at him, her eyes were red and glassy. Raw.

"Em? What's wrong?" He set the toolbox down and crossed to her without thinking.

She shook her head, quick and tight. "Nothing."

"Emily..." He brushed a knuckle gently under her cheek, catching a tear. "That's not nothing."

She gave him a weak, watery smile. "I'll be okay."

He hated how helpless he felt. He could build a deck, rewire a room, fix damn near anything. Except this.

"I'm just going to sit outside for a bit," she said softly, already turning away.

He didn't follow. Not yet. The screen door creaked behind her, then clicked shut. He stood there for a moment, heart pounding, unsure whether he should've pushed more... or said less.

He picked up the toolbox he had carried in. There were a few minor projects that could be fixed, cabinet doors that needed tightening; a floorboard that had come loose. He may not know what to do with Emily at the moment, but he knew what he could do about her house.

• • • •

EMILY SLOWLY ROCKED on the porch swing, the faded wood creaking beneath her. Inside, she heard Noah moving around. Quiet footsteps, the low thud of a hammer, a gentle scrape as something was shifted or repaired. He'd always been that way. Never one to stand still when something was broken. He had to fix it. Even now, when the broken thing wasn't his.

The breeze off the gulf rustled the magnolia leaves. She closed her eyes, letting the warm air brush against her face. The scent of salt and sun-bleached wood filled her lungs.

A memory rose, uninvited but clear as day.

Graduation announcements had come in. She'd laid the packet on Grams' counter, smiling like her heart wasn't cracking open from missing her parents. Answered every "How was your day?" like it didn't ache. Then she'd slipped away to the beach.

Noah had found her there, barefoot in the sand.

"What's up?" he'd asked, like he didn't already know.

"Nothing."

He hadn't pushed. Just walked beside her, quiet and steady. Let her talk about school, baseball, Carly and Benjamin. Anything but graduation. It was like he'd known exactly what she needed.

The hammering stopped. A few moments later, Noah stepped onto the porch. He sat beside her on the swing and let the silence settle between them.

"I'm scared," Emily whispered.

He turned to her. "Of what?"

"I don't know," she admitted. "Everything."

He leaned forward, resting his elbows on his knees. "Em, you've got nothing to be scared of from me. I'd never hurt you. Not ever."

Her hand moved to her hip before she could stop the action, rubbing the spot as if it might still be bruised. "I know."

Noah's gaze followed the motion. "What happened to your hip?"

She didn't answer right away. The words took effort, like dragging them through mud.

"It was Eddie," she said finally. "I picked up an extra shift at the café, came home smelling like burgers and burnt coffee. He was already drunk. Accused me of cheating."

Noah froze.

"He grabbed me. Shoved me into the cabinets. I hit my hip on the corner."

She gave a bitter laugh. "Funny thing is, when I pushed him back, he fell. That stunned him more than anything I said. After that, I locked my bedroom door every night. Until I left."

Noah stood and walked to the porch railing. His back was to her, but she could see his shoulders drawn tight, hands gripping the wood.

After a moment, he spoke. "I'm sorry, Em. I'm so damn sorry."

"I filed for divorce today," she said.

He turned to look at her. "Good. That's good."

She swallowed. "I don't think I can do this. With you. I mean. We both know something's there. But I have so much baggage. I can't be what you need. Not right now."

He came back to her, crouched in front of her until their eyes met. "Emily, I don't want anything from you that you're not ready to give. And when you get to be our age, we all come with baggage. The trick is finding someone willing to help carry it."

She blinked back sudden tears.

He smiled, gentle. "How about this? Tomorrow, let's go to New Orleans. I need to pick up some stuff for Snapper's. You need supplies for the house. Seeing progress might help. As for the rest...we'll figure it out when you're ready."

A slow smile tugged at her lips. "You're awesome, you know."

"I don't know about that," he said, and actually blushed. "But, I want you to know you don't have to carry your baggage alone."

He kissed her forehead, soft and lingering, then slid onto the swing beside her. His arm stretched out along the back, and she leaned into him without hesitation. His arm curled around her shoulders to cradle her.

They didn't need to speak. The porch swing rocked gently, the sky tinted with the last light of day, and for the first time in a long while, Emily let herself believe she wasn't in this alone.

• • • •

THE HUM OF TIRES ON gravel pulled Noah's gaze from the small block of wood in his hands. He sat on the deck of his houseboat, a pocketknife in one hand, cedar curls gathering at his feet.

He looked up in time to see Glinda's truck ease to a stop near the dock. She climbed out, holding a foil-covered casserole dish like it was a peace offering.

She called out, "I brought shrimp étouffée. And don't try to tell me you've already eaten."

He chuckled, taking the dish from her. "Thanks. Haven't had anything hot all day."

"I figured as much." She followed him up onto the houseboat's deck and settled into a chair facing the water. "Sadie around?"

"Inside. She got into a pelican standoff earlier and decided a nap was safer."

Glinda gave a satisfied nod. "Girl's got sense."

Noah returned with two glasses of tea and sat beside her. The sun was beginning its slow slide toward the horizon, warm and heavy on their shoulders.

They sipped in silence for a minute before Glinda spoke.

"Emily told me she went to the attorney today."

He nodded once.

Glinda watched him, not unkindly. "That's a big step for her."

"Yeah."

"But also a shift for you, isn't it?"

He didn't answer right away.

"I don't know what it means yet," he said finally. "She's going through a lot. I just want to be there for her."

"You always were," Glinda said

He looked down at the glass in his hand.

"I want her safe. I want her to realize she doesn't have to go through this alone. Past that...."

Glinda didn't press. "And if she ever wants more from you?"

He looked out toward the water. "Then I'll be here. And we'll figure it out."

She smiled gently, reaching over to squeeze his arm. "Good. Just don't forget you're allowed to have a heart in this, too."

They sat for a moment in comfortable silence, looking out at the water.

"We're going to New Orleans tomorrow," he added. "Picking up supplies for her place. And Snapper's."

"Sounds like a good trip," she said. "Progress. Paint. Maybe a beignet or two."

Glinda stood with a sigh. "Noah? Let me know if you need anything. Not just hammer-and-nails stuff, either."

He nodded. "Thanks, Glinda."

She headed for her truck, the setting sun casting long shadows behind her as Noah stood alone with the scent of étouffée, salty gulf air, and possibility.

# Chapter Fourteen

Emily hesitated at the end of the dock, twisting a lock of hair around her finger. This was a bad idea. A terrible idea. She and Noah were going to New Orleans to get supplies to finish the house. It was a town famous for romance with its cozy restaurants, carriage rides, and history steeped in mystery. Her last trip there had been with Eddie, and what a disaster that had been!

The door swung open, and Noah greeted her with a warm smile and a thermal mug of coffee.

"Coffee? Handsome and prepared?" she teased, wrapping her hands around the mug like it was a lifeline. "Where have you been all my life?"

"Right here, darlin'," he said, with a wink that sent her stomach flipping in a way that had nothing to do with caffeine.

"So, Ms. Emily. You ready?"

"Yep."

"Let's go." He walked to her side of the truck and held the door open. Always the gentleman. *I could get used to this.*

Noah had the station set to rock music, and he entertained her with stories about the songs. He impressed Emily with his musical knowledge. He knew the stories about who wrote the songs and why they were written.

A particularly sad song came on the radio, and it reminded her of life before she had run away and came home to the coast. The song echoed how utterly drained she felt.

"Noah?" Emily kept her gaze on the passing trees. "Have you ever been too tired to even think straight? Like, you're going through the motions, but you're not... there?"

He glanced at her, eyes soft. "Yeah. After my last tour overseas. Everything felt like quicksand."

She nodded. "That's what it was like with Eddie. I wasn't living. I was surviving."

He said nothing, just reached over and adjusted the volume knob so her voice didn't have to fight the music.

"I remember the last time we came to New Orleans," she went on, quieter now. "He got drunk, as usual. I was half-dragging him down Bourbon Street, trying not to cry or cuss or both. When we got back to the room, he collapsed on the bed and pulled me down with him. Gross slobbery kiss, heavy arm, the whole thing. When I pulled away, he called me a cow. A fat cow."

Noah muttered a curse under his breath.

"I slept in the other bed that night. Curled up in a ball. Waited for morning."

She turned back to the window. "So yeah, today's going to be different. Sunshine. Good company. No ghosts." Then she smiled a little. "Except the ones in the French Quarter."

She glanced at him. He smiled that gentle Noah smile, and she returned it.

"Today, I don't want to worry about Eddie or my marriage, or money, or what I want to do with my life. The sun is shining, the air is warm, and the company is excellent. I want to enjoy myself, if only for today."

Noah grinned. "As you wish."

· · · ·

NOAH FOUND A PARKING spot on Canal Street, near the old brewery that had been converted into a shopping mall. It was still mid-morning, so they made their way through the already half-busy French Quarter to Café Du Monde. Emily breathed in the fragrance of the strong coffee. Pigeons stalked customers, just waiting for bits of the soft beignets to hit the ground. Emily found a small iron table near the street while Noah went to the counter.

Emily watched people pass while she waited. All kinds of people made their way to New Orleans. There were the obviously international tourists with their cameras and guidebooks. There were the locals bustling about from the French Market, or to work. She could see street performers and artists setting up around Jackson Square. She saw the tarot card readers. Maybe she would get her cards read later. The future had to be better than the past; she thought with a smile.

Noah returned and placed a steaming cup of coffee and a plate piled high with powdery beignets in the middle of the table.

"Yum," she said before even tasting them. She had often contemplated learning how to make them, but knew that they would never taste like this at home. Part of the flavor here was the local atmosphere.

"Carly has a ball here," Noah said, as he nodded at a group of colorful characters.

"Why's that?" Emily asked.

"She sits and creates stories in her head about all the people. She has her little notebook out and writes notes. She is wasting her talent," he said.

"But isn't she writing now?"

"She's got more potential than that. What she's working on is funny, but it only scratches the surface of what she can do. I believe she's afraid of delving too deeply.

"I keep meaning to read what she's written, but she never brings it to me. I think she brings some to Daniel."

"She lets Daniel read them sometimes. You've gotta nudge her. She has a lot on her plate right now with Snapper's, and that guy in Biloxi."

"I can imagine," Emily said.

Noah reached across the table and ran fingers slowly across her cheek, "Sugar," he explained when she raised an eyebrow. His eyes narrowed. Then he nodded toward the empty plate.

"You ready?" he asked, standing and offering his hand. "New Orleans is waiting."

They strolled down Bourbon Street, weaving through crowds and bursts of music spilling from open doors. Men in the doorways called out deals, promising the best drinks and the wildest nights. A blues band wailed from one bar; an 80s hair-metal cover band shredded in the next. At a place boasting a bucking whale instead of a mechanical bull, they stopped for a drink and stayed long enough to laugh at the riders being flung to the floor one after another.

"Grace plays in one of these places," Noah said.

"Is that right?" Emily said. "That's so cool!"

"Yeah, one night we'll come watch her play. We're trying to plan a night out over here, anyway."

"That sounds like fun," Emily said.

"Now, want to venture out to the French Market?" he asked her. "Do some shopping? I wouldn't mind picking out a few early Christmas presents. You can help me see if I can find something for Carly. I'm no good at that."

"I can do that," she smiled. "Christmas is my favorite holiday. Christmas and New Year's."

"Really?"

"Yes. Christmas always seems like such a time for miracles. Then you have New Year's, a time to let go of the past and look forward to the future."

"Seems to me like you're already celebrating a kind of New Year's," Noah said.

Emily pondered that for a moment. "I guess you're right."

Noah smiled and placed his hand on her elbow, guiding her through the sporadic crowds of people.

Suddenly, Emily stopped as a poster caught her eye.

"Southern Louisiana Culinary Institute's 25th Annual Seafood Cook-Off. Grand prize $25,000. Hmmmm." Emily said.

"Want to check it out?" Noah asked.

"Yes."

He opened the door and bowed slightly. "After you, my dear."

She felt the smile light up her face as they walked into the reception area.

"Can I help you?" the woman behind the desk asked.

"Yes," Noah said. "We're considering entering the cook-off you have coming up. Do you have any information about that?"

"Yes, I do."

She handed him some pamphlets. "This should give you all the rules and guidelines. It even has some websites where you can view finalist's recipes to have an idea of what has won in the past."

Emily stared at the flyer, her heart pounding. Twenty-five thousand dollars. That could change everything. A cheap food truck? A van? She didn't say a word. But Noah was already moving toward the door. "After you, my dear," he said with a wink.

As they stepped back out into the sunlight, Emily couldn't stop smiling. Suddenly, the future seemed wide open.

• • • •

PURCHASES FROM THE French Market in hand, Noah and Emily wandered back through the French Quarter. The air was thick with music and the scent of red beans, rice, and other local favorites. As they passed Jackson Square, Emily slowed near the row of tarot readers.

Noah caught her glance. "How about we get a reading?"

Emily hesitated, then smiled. "Why not?"

"You pick."

They circled the square slowly, inspecting setups like shoppers at a farmer's market. After a loop around, Emily tugged Noah's sleeve. "This one." She pointed to an older man with a bushy gray beard seated beneath a faded purple umbrella. His table was small but neat, a burning stick of incense curling smoke into the air. A sign read: *Tarot Readings by Edmund* in ornate lettering.

"Gotcha," Noah said, leading the way.

Edmund looked up with warm, knowing eyes. "What can I do for you two today?"

"The lady would like a reading," Noah said.

Emily gave him a look. "If I do, you do."

"I can live with that. Ladies first."

Edmund slid a worn deck across the table. "Shuffle until you feel like stopping."

Emily took the cards and gave them a few thoughtful shuffles before handing them back. He laid out a cross-shaped pattern and flipped the first card.

"Ah," Edmund murmured. "Change. You've come to a crossroads recently. Big decisions. You're not just rearranging your life. You're rebuilding it from the foundation."

Emily's breath caught slightly. She didn't look at Noah, but she felt him watching her.

Edmund pointed to another card. "The Fool. New journey's ahead."

Emily let out a short laugh. "That's right."

Edmund smiled, flipping another card, the Sun. "This one's my favorite. A new day. A clean slate. Happiness on the horizon. You're stepping into a brighter chapter."

She bit her lip; the words hitting deeper than expected.

He tapped the final card. "One thing still lingers. Unfinished business. A ghost, metaphorical or otherwise."

Emily's smile faltered.

"My advice?" Edmund continued. "Don't be afraid of the light just because the dark lasted too long."

Emily nodded. "Okay."

She turned to Noah. "Your turn."

Noah shuffled the deck with the same measured calm he brought to everything else. When he was done, Edmund laid out the cards in a similar cross. His brows lifted.

"Interesting."

Emily leaned forward, curious.

"You've been through so much," Edmund said. "Pain buried so deep you stopped noticing it. But it's still there, my friend. You've been carrying it quietly for too long."

Noah didn't respond, but his fingers twitched where they rested on the edge of the table.

"There's a door opening. Something or someone from your past is coming back. Unfinished, unresolved."

Emily's stomach flipped. Could he mean Eddie too?

Edmund looked at Noah closely, "you've made some peace for yourself. But sometimes peace comes from finally facing the thing you're running from."

Noah shifted. Emily saw the flicker of tension in his jaw.

"You two," Edmund said, gesturing between them, "you're walking parallel paths. You've both been caretakers for people. You put others first and forgot that you're important too."

They sat silently for a beat too long.

"The good news?" Edmund flipped one last card. "You've both started over. There's potential here. But only if you don't keep pushing people away."

He sat back. "Any questions?"

Noah shook his head, eyes distant.

"Me either," Emily said quietly.

Noah pulled out his wallet and passed the man a few bills. "Thanks."

"Good luck," Edmund said. "You've already done the hard part. Now don't be afraid to enjoy what comes next."

As they stepped back onto the sidewalk, Edmund's words haunted her. Unfinished business, ghosts?

Beside her, Noah bumped her shoulder gently. "Lunch? Then we grab those supplies?"

She nodded, glancing back once at the square, where Edmund had already lit a new stick of incense and was shuffling the cards for the next reader. "Yeah. Let's do that."

• • • •

NOAH PULLED TO A STOP in front of her house. "Had a good time today?" he asked after they got out of the truck.

"Yes, I did."

He looked toward the boat. "I want to show you something."

She was quiet as she followed him across the beach to the boat. Wanting to ease her nerves, he offered her what he hoped was a reassuring smile.

He led her to the top deck of the houseboat. One of his favorite spots on the boat. "I'll be right back." He said before going below for blankets and drinks.

"Come see," he said, patting the chair beside him. "Trust me, Emily."

She hesitated, arms crossed, eyes flicking between the blanket and the seat. But after a moment, she stepped forward. Her nearness made his pulse jump.

As she sat, he pulled the blanket around them both and handed her the drink. "There we go," he said, his voice low. "Nice view, huh?"

The stars spilled across the sky like sparkling jewels. There was a light breeze that made it chilly, but not uncomfortable. It was as if the entire universe was visible above them.

"This is beautiful," she said.

"You should see it during a meteor shower."

They sipped in silence for a moment. Then, softly, she said, "Thank you for today. I didn't realize how much I needed... everything."

He tilted his head toward her. "Beignets, fortune-telling, and a potential cook-off? The essentials."

She laughed. "No, really. It was the first time in a while I didn't feel... haunted."

"Even with the ghosts in the French Quarter?"

She elbowed him gently. "Those don't count."

They both chuckled, then quiet fell again.

"That tarot reader," she said, "he said I needed to stop being afraid."

Noah nodded slowly. "He wasn't wrong."

She looked The way her smile, when it came, always felt like a small victory. over. "You think I'm afraid?"

"I believe you've had reason to be. But, you're getting stronger day by day. That says a lot more."

She gave a soft, thoughtful hum. "He got to you, too, didn't he?"

"Yeah. He said that I push people away. And I guess I do. I guess I've always thought I had to be the strong one."

Her voice dropped. "You don't push me away."

He glanced at her. "No," he said. "I don't."

*Not yet.*

His phone buzzed on the small table beside the chairs. He leaned forward, checked the screen: a voicemail from Kevin Daniels.

He frowned, tapped the screen off, and left it face down.

Emily raised an eyebrow. "Everything okay?"

"Yeah," he said, keeping his voice level. "A check-in from an old friend. It can wait until tomorrow."

She didn't press. Instead, she leaned back into the chair, close enough that her shoulder brushed his.

"I still don't know what the future looks like," she said. "But tonight? I like this."

He reached over, threading his fingers with hers beneath the blanket. "This, this is good."

The stars above shimmered like scattered promises. The boat rocked gently beneath them, the water lapping against the dock in a slow, steady rhythm. And for a little while, he let himself forget the voicemail left unheard.

# Chapter Fifteen

H*e ducked behind the cover of a building. His rifle was heavy in his arms. Sweat dripped down his forehead underneath the heat of his helmet. He could hear shots in the distance. He heard a noise behind him. Instinctively, he tensed.*

*SNAP!*

Noah's eyes popped open. His heart was pounding, and sweat was dripping down his forehead into his eyes. He looked over to see Emily still sleeping. Grateful that he hadn't woken her up, he ran a shaky hand over his brow. He swung his legs over the side of the lounge chair and leaned his head over, cradling his face in his hands.

*Breathe In. Breathe Out. Breathe In. Breathe Out.*

He repeated the mantra in his head over and over until his pulse slowed, and breathing evened. He glanced at the cell phone. 4:00 am. He wouldn't be going back to sleep. He went downstairs to the bedroom. He shrugged on some sweatpants and running shoes. He had to get out. Get away. It was time for a run. He whistled for Sadie. Together, they ran down the beach.

While running, he cleared his mind. He concentrated on the stars glittering in the sky and reflected on the water. He listened to the waves splash against the shore, washing from his mind the echoes of gunfire.

*Breathe In. Breathe Out.*

He ran until his heart pounded and his lungs hurt. Then he stopped and lifted his head to the now rising sun.

*Breathe in Breathe Out.*

He took a deep breath. His demons exorcised for now. He headed back to his boat. It was time for a shower and coffee.

• • • •

THE PHONE RANG, AND Noah walked out of the bedroom, toweling his hair.

"Good God, who is calling at this hour?"

It was Kevin Douglas. No need to put off the inevitable. He swiped to answer.

"Devereaux?" As soon as he heard the voice, his heart started pounding.

"Yes."

"This is Douglas."

Staff Sergeant Kevin Douglas was from La Fleur Parish and had served with Noah on that last tour in Iraq. He had been Noah's superior and part of the experience that still gave him nightmares. Noah felt a familiar tightening in his gut. Restless, he paced the small kitchen.

"Douglas. How are you?"

"I'm great. I'm heading home soon for leave, thought we'd have a beer. How are you doing?"

"I'm hanging in there."

"Will call you soon when I know more. That inn still open?"

"Yes."

"I'll get a room there. Will talk to you soon."

*Breathe in. Breathe out.*

"Noah?" Emily's voice was soft.

"What?" he snapped, more harshly than he meant to. He kept his back to her, jaw clenched.

"I don't mean to pry," she said. Her voice was steadier now, but quieter too. "I just... you looked like you could use someone."

He didn't respond. Couldn't. Not without unraveling in front of her.

She waited a moment longer, then said, "I'll see you at Gram's later."

He nodded, barely.

As she turned, her footsteps hesitated near the door. "You don't always have to be strong for me, you know."

The door clicked shut behind her.

• • • •

EMILY SAT ON THE PORCH steps of her grandparents' house, knees drawn up and chin resting on them, waiting for Noah like she had as a teenager. Only now, she wasn't a girl with a crush and a head full of daydreams. She was a grown woman, trying not to over-analyze the sharp edge in his voice that morning... or the way he'd avoided her eyes. She hoped it wouldn't be awkward when he showed up.

She glanced back at the house. Her house. It still felt strange to call it that. So much of it still whispered with her grandparents' presence. But soon, it would be hers. Noah had promised they'd start with the roof today, then tackle the ceilings and windows. She could move in after the roof and windows were fixed. It wouldn't be long until she was sleeping in that old room of hers.

Her own place. She smiled. Technically, she had her own place now, but it wasn't really HERS. She hadn't picked out any of the décor. It didn't have any personal touches.

Emily had gone to the bank a few days ago and been pleasantly surprised. With interest, she had something else she hadn't had before. A cushion. If budgeted correctly, she would have enough to fix the house up, and put some up for a crisis, like a divorce. With no mortgage or rent to worry about anymore, she had time to figure out what she wanted to do permanently. She knew she wanted to cook, but what? Catering, own her own restaurant? Would she get enough local business during the off season? With a catering company, she would be mobile to travel.

Noah's truck rounded the corner and pulled to a stop in the driveway, cutting her musings short. He climbed out of the driver's side and Joey out of the passenger's. Noah stood in front of his truck and smiled as two more vehicles rolled in. Emily's mouth dropped open as Ryder, Carly, Glinda, and Daniel all filed into her small yard.

Glinda came up and hugged her, "C'mon girl. Let's get started. We'll get you all fixed up and in this house in no time."

Emily's lip quivered, and her eyes filled with tears. "I don't know what to say."

"You don't have to say anything at all, girl." She linked an arm around Emily's. "Come on y'all, let's see what we need to do."

Glinda pointed at Noah. "You get those guys going, and we'll see what we need to get done in the house. Let's get Emily back where she belongs."

• • • •

HOURS LATER, EMILY sank down onto the porch swing, exhausted. The roof was repaired enough that rain was no longer a problem. There was still some work to be done there though. The rest of the group was in the kitchen, finishing some clean up. In the midst of the chaos, Emily had escaped outside for some quiet.

"You okay?" Noah asked as he too, came outside. He joined her on the swing. He stretched an arm out across the back of the swing, almost touching her shoulders, but not quite. Emily made no move to scoot away.

"I'm good. Just needed to rest for a minute."

"I understand that."

"We had some good times here," he said.

"We did," and Emily thought of her first kiss. Their first kiss. After the night at the dance, Noah had come over and they had sat outside on this very swing. His arm around her was almost the same as it was now. He was more self-assured now, and the movement was more natural than it had been then.

She wondered if he was remembering it too. One look in his smoky eyes and she knew exactly what he was thinking. Slowly, he leaned forward. She moved to meet him. She had just closed her eyes when they were interrupted.

"Oh now, don't let me stop you," Ryder's voice drawled from the open doorway. "But the rest are coming outside."

Noah cursed, and Emily moved to the end of the swing. Moments later, the porch was filled with people.

Carly wiped sweat off her forehead and flopped down in the porch's shade. "Damn, I need a drink."

"Noah's got some bottled water in the ice chest," Emily said, pointing to the red and white cooler Noah had slid onto the porch earlier.

"Not water. I need an ice cold beer," she said, groaning and stretching. "You know what else we need?"

"What?" Emily asked.

"A bar crawl. We worked hard today. We need to get out and have some fun. What do you guys think?" she asked.

"I'm always up for a night out," Ryder said.

"I'm in," Joey said.

"Daniel? Be a D. D?" Carly asked.

"I will."

"Me too," Noah said.

"Sounds like a deal then," Carly said. "Meet at the Inn in an hour? That should give us all time to freshen up."

Everyone nodded; Glinda surprised Emily by nodding too. Seems like everyone was all in. Emily let herself go with the flow, determined to enjoy it.

• • • •

AT THE INN, THE GROUP split into two vehicles. Emily rode with Carly, Glinda, and Daniel, while Noah took Joey and Ryder in Joey's jeep. Ryder gave the SUV full of women a lingering glance but slid into the backseat of the jeep, loyalty winning out.

Soon, they were pulling into a parking lot. The Wild Wahoo, the sign proclaimed in huge flamingo pink letters. An enormous fish also adorned the sign. A few cars littered the parking lot, a slow night it seemed, but it was Sunday, and the Saints had played a noon game.

The bartender glanced up from her phone, clearly not expecting a crowd this size on a Sunday night. But her smile indicated she was happy for the extra business.

Carly claimed the jukebox and declared it "80s Night." Emily braced herself as she took a seat with the others at a small round table. Carly returned, shots in hand.

"What is this?" Emily asked, eyeing the liquid suspiciously.

"A Carly Bomb," Carly said.

"What's in it?"

"Don't ask. Just toast."

"To friends!" Carly shouted.

"Wake me up before you go go..." played from the jukebox. Noah, Joey, and Ryder groaned.

"Seriously, Carly?" Ryder asked. "Surely you can think of better 80s music than that."

He stood up and grabbed some dollars from his wallet. "I can't take this. How are you supposed to dance to this?" He patted Carly on the shoulder. "Come see. Let's go play some good music."

Before Carly could respond, a woman in a leopard print top and penciled-on brows strutted over.

"Well, hello, Daniel," she purred.

Daniel winced. "Hi, Cecile."

She plopped herself between the guys, claiming a spot like it owed her rent. "Which one of these cuties are free tonight?" she asked.

Three sets of eyes silently begged for rescue.

Glinda patted Daniel's knee. "This one's taken."

Emily followed suit. "Noah's with me."

Cecile pivoted to Joey, leaned in slowly, and licked his arm like a cat.

Joey blinked, frozen in horror.

"You're young," Cecile said, eyes twinkling. "I like stamina."

Her hand slid under the table. Joey jerked like he'd touched a live wire.

"Joey, dance with me," Emily blurted. "You don't mind, do you, Noah?"

Noah, lips twitching, shook his head. "Go ahead, sweetheart."

"Thank you," Joey whispered as they walked to the dance floor.

The song was over soon, and Emily shook her head as the familiar beat of the old Macarena song filled the bar.

She was not dancing to that. She shook her head at Joey. He was on his own now.

Joey laughed as they walked back to their seats. Cecile had moved on to the next table. Her eyes still traveled back to the guys, and Emily knew the cougar would probably circle back.

Carly returned with more shots. Emily sighed. This was going to be a long night.

A new face joined them. An older man with bleached teeth and too much cologne. "I'm Richard," he said, offering Carly a hand. She shook it, then winced.

"Ow."

"Sorry. Karate reflexes. Must've accidentally hit a pressure point."

"How do you accidentally do that?" Carly asked, rubbing her hand.

Richard launched into a demonstration, hands slicing the air with exaggerated hi-yahs.

Noah stiffened beside Emily. She felt the tension in his shoulders but saw he was watching Carly, not intervening. Not yet.

"I think I need another drink," Emily muttered.

"I'll join you," Noah said quickly.

As they waited at the bar, a fast Cajun two-step rolled through the speakers. Emily looked for Ryder. Before she could spot him, someone grabbed her rear.

Her head whipped around. Noah's hands were still on the bar. Cecile.

"You've got a nice butt," Cecile said cheerfully.

Emily latched onto Noah's arm. "My husband says that all the time. Right, honey?"

Noah barely contained a laugh. "The best," he said, patting her backside.

Emily stared, wide-eyed. "Let's... go back to the table."

His hand slid to her waist as they returned.

Back at the table, Richard was still performing air-katas.

"I don't need self-defense," Carly said. "I've got wasp spray. Much more effective than pepper spray. Wanna see?"

"Let me show you anyway," Richard insisted.

Ryder returned just in time to help. "Carly, I need backup at the jukebox."

"Coming."

Seconds later, a familiar beat kicked in.

"Everybody was kung fu fighting..."

Emily snorted, then full-on choked, spraying her drink across the table right onto Richard's pristine white shirt.

"I'm so sorry," she said, still laughing.

He glared at Emily, wiping the tight white shirt with a napkin.

"I'm so sorry," Emily said, still laughing.

"Let's go check out what's going on at 31," Carly said. "I think it's time for a change in scenery."

• • • •

BAR 31 SAT OUTSIDE the St. Andrew Parish line, a larger, livelier spot than the Wahoo. Cars packed the gravel lot, drawn in by the lure of karaoke.

Inside, someone warbled through a painful rendition of Patsy Cline's "Crazy." The group snagged a dark corner table, hoping to blend in this time.

Noah and Carly returned with drinks. Soft drinks for him and Daniel, beers and mixed drinks for the rest. Carly also plunked down another tray of shots with a devious grin.

"To friends!" she cheered. "I'm going to sing," she added, eyes on Emily. "Wanna join me?"

"Um. No," Emily said.

"Oh, you're no fun," Carly teased.

"You go ahead. I'll enjoy the show from here."

"Fine. You have any requests?" Carly said to the group.

"Something not stupid," Ryder said.

"How about Hammer Time?" Joey said. "That's a horrible song you haven't tortured us with yet."

"I can't do the dance," Carly said. "If I were wearing my 80s pants, you bet your sweet ass I'd sing it."

Joey shook his head.

She scribbled her song choice and disappeared to the DJ booth.

Emily sat back and sipped the drink. Carly was definitely a handful. The next karaoke performer was up, and he began singing an old country song.

"C'mon, Em. Let's dance," Noah said, nudging her arm.

She smiled at him, "Sure."

She smiled and rose. Carly grabbed Joey for a spin, and Ryder charmed a woman near the bar.

As they moved, Emily soaked in Noah's nearness. The quiet strength in the way he held her, the warmth of his hand resting just above her waist. The low hum of chatter and clinking glasses faded beneath the beat of the music and the scent of his cologne. Something woodsy and clean that made her want to lean in closer.

She stumbled slightly as he shifted, brushing her foot.

"You okay?" he asked, his arm tightening around her.

She looked up, meeting his eyes. "Yeah," she said, breath catching. "I'm good. Maybe a little distracted."

He gave a small, lopsided smile. "Sorry about this morning. I've been meaning to say that all day."

Her gaze dropped for a moment, before returning to his. "It's okay. I get it. I mean... I don't, not all of it. But I understand enough."

He nodded, his thumb lightly brushing her back. "I didn't mean to shut you out."

"I know." Her voice was softer now. "You're not the only one figuring things out."

Noah didn't answer right away. But the way he pulled her a fraction closer said enough.

The song ended too soon. Back at the table, Carly's name boomed from the DJ's mic.

"Now singing... Miss Carly Devereaux with 'Jose Cuervo.'"

Carly strutted to the mic like it was a stage on Bourbon Street. Her vocals were... enthusiastic, and what she lacked in pitch, she made up for in crowd-pleasing antics. She flirted, winked, and hopped onto the bar, hamming it up to the crowd's delight.

The door to the bar opened and two police officers walked in. One wore a St. Andrew Parish Sheriff's uniform, one a city. In the dark, it was hard to tell what city, but Emily assumed it was Pointe Shade, the town where 31 was located.

Carly faltered, and the bar went quiet. One officer, the younger one in the city uniform, walked up to the bar.

"Oh, go ahead, don't let us interrupt you," he said.

"You know what?" Carly said. "I think I just lost my voice."

She walked to where Ryder was still standing, and he gave her a hand down from the bar.

The officers stalked through the place, looking at everyone as if looking for prey.

The one in the St. Andrew uniform joined them at the table. He turned a chair backward and straddled it and turned to Carly. "Nice performance."

"Thanks," Carly said, stiffly polite.

"What brings y'all out tonight?"

"We *were* enjoying ourselves," Glinda said, shooting him a pointed glance.

Emily stifled a smile.

His attention was still on Carly. His smile sharpened. "Name?"

"Carly."

"Carly, that's a very nice name for such a beautiful lady."

Emily watched as Carly glanced down at his hands. She noticed the grey wedding band when Carly did.

"And your wife?" Carly asked.

"Well, what she doesn't know won't hurt her, will it?" he flashed a smile that didn't match the dark gleam in his eyes.

Emily's stomach twisted.

"I'm Officer Mouton, by the way. Denis Mouton." he said, holding a hand out to Carly. He eyed her up and down. "It's a pleasure."

Emily watched as indecision danced across Carly's face. Emily wasn't sure if Carly was going to shake his hand or slap him.

Carly held out a hand, but said nothing. She simply looked him in the eye silently.

The other officer returned. Nothing to report.

"I'll see you soon," he said with a wink. To Emily, it sounded like a threat, and she shivered.

After the officers left, Carly muttered, "I think I just threw up in my mouth."

"Let's wait a minute before we leave," Daniel said. "Give 'em time to clear the area."

They agreed. No one wanted a bogus traffic stop.

The mood had shifted. When they got back to Bon Chance, Daniel and Glinda called it a night. The rest wandered into Snapper's.

Carly passed out shots before hitting the jukebox.

"Play something you can really dance to," Ryder said. "I haven't really gotten to dance all night."

"Ryder, who you gonna dance with? Carly can't dance to anything!" Joey teased.

Carly turned and stuck her tongue out at the two. "How about some Wayne Toups?"

"Sure," Ryder said.

Noah settled onto the stool beside her and smiled. "Having fun?"

"I am, actually. Didn't really care for that run-in with the cop, though."

He grimaced, "Yeah, I know. There's been some rumblings about cover-ups and corruption over there since Mouton took office."

"Take My Hand...." the popular Cajun song played.

"Dance?" Noah asked.

"Sure."

Noah led Emily to the dance floor, holding her closer than earlier. She relaxed in his arms, enjoying the feel of him.

Emily looked over to see Carly and Joey sharing a dance. Emily felt bad for Joey. And Carly. Maybe a few dances would clear the cloudy air around them and they could see how much they cared about each other.

Noah pulled her closer, leaned down, and placed a kiss on the top of her head. Emily smiled. Against her better judgment, her heart melted. This was not a good idea.

The song ended, and they resumed their seats. Carly soon had another round of shots lined up.

"To friends!" they all toasted.

Noah scooted his seat closer and wrapped an arm around Emily and she leaned into his embrace.

• • • •

NOAH GUIDED EMILY HOME.

One. Two. Three... she recited in her head as she counted footsteps, trying to walk a straight line.

She should not have done that last round of shots. Or the last three rounds of shots. She was grateful for Noah's steadying arm. He laughed as she swayed one way, then the other.

He helped her up the stairs, took the key, and opened the door.

Noah shook his head, still smiling.

"C'mere, *cher*." he led her to the bedroom. He pulled the sheets back and patted the bed. "Climb in."

Emily obeyed, and all but fell into the bed.

Noah tucked the blanket around her and leaned over. He eyed her lips, and Emily bit her bottom lip. His eyes darkened. He was going to kiss her.

Emily closed her eyes.

His lips were warm against her forehead.

Emily's eyes popped open. He saw the question in them.

"When I kiss you the first time, *cher*, I want to be sure you know what you're doing." He kissed her forehead again and chuckled. "And that you'll actually remember it."

He smoothed her hair away from her forehead.

"Good night, Emily," he said, and turned off the lamp beside the bed. Emily was already out by the time he quietly closed the front door as he left.

# Chapter Sixteen

"*When I kiss you for the first time...*"

Noah could still feel the ghost of her lips under his. Almost. Just a breath apart. He'd kissed her forehead instead.

"Well, the first time again," he'd added, trying to keep it light. "I want to be sure you remember it."

She'd smiled, all soft and sleepy, and he'd wanted nothing more than to stay. But he didn't.

And now, the morning sun continued to rise over the gulf. He sat behind the wheel of his truck and rubbed at the tension that had taken up permanent residence in his neck.

He hadn't really slept and went for a run before dawn, showered, tried to focus. None of it had helped.

Too many things were crowding his mind. Kevin's phone call and future arrival. The looming soft opening at Snapper's. The memory of Benjamin surfacing without warning in that pre-dawn silence.

He told himself he'd done the right thing. Emily deserved a clear-headed kiss.

But the way she'd looked at him stuck with him like a song that wouldn't fade.

He leaned forward, resting his forearms on the steering wheel, and exhaled slowly through his nose. Everything felt off-kilter.

A sharp knock at the window made him flinch. He cursed under his breath and looked up to see Carly peering in, one eyebrow raised like she already had a comment locked and loaded.

"You planning on living in that truck," she said.

He cracked the window. "Just thinking."

"Don't hurt yourself," she teased, but her tone was softer than usual. "You helping today? We have a few more things to wrap up before the soft opening."

"I'll be in soon."

She gave a little nod and turned away.

Noah watched the inn come to life across the street, sunlight glinting off the windows. He knew Emily would be waking up about now.

And he had no idea if she'd remember what didn't happen between them. Or if she'd wish it had.

· · · ·

EMILY GROANED BEFORE her eyes even opened.

Her head throbbed in sync with her heartbeat. A sharp, pulsing pain that radiated from her temples down to her molars. The sunlight filtering through the curtains sliced across the room like a blade, stabbing her right between the eyes. Her mouth was dry and her tongue was like sandpaper.

A hangover. Classic. Rookie mistake.

She peeled one eye open and blinked at the ceiling. The room was too bright, too quiet, and still tilted slightly to the left.

And then it hit her.

Noah's voice, low and warm in the dim light.

Her breath caught. God, had she actually bitten her lip?

Yes. Yes, she had.

And he'd noticed.

His gaze had darkened, and for one heartbeat-long moment, the world had stilled. She'd closed her eyes, lips parted just slightly, the entire universe leaning forward to meet him halfway...

And his kiss had landed on her forehead instead.

"When I kiss you the first time, *cher*, I want to be sure you know what you're doing."

Emily groaned and flopped back onto the bed, dragging the sheet up to her chin like it could block out the entire night. The memory replayed in loops, getting sharper with every rotation.

She remembered it.

Oh, she remembered it too well.

The distant buzz of her phone made her jump. She groped blindly across the nightstand, knocking over a water bottle and a half-full bottle of ibuprofen before her fingers closed around the screen.

**Carly**: You still coming to help at Snapper's today?

Emily stared at the text for a long moment before typing back: I'll be there soon.

She set the phone down and exhaled. That almost kiss hadn't been nothing.

It had been everything.

And she had absolutely no idea what the hell to do with it.

• • • •

EMILY WIPED DOWN THE counter, the scent of lemon cleaner mixing with fresh-cut wood. She liked being here, even in the chaos of last-minute prep for the soft opening. Snapper's felt full of possibilities. Like a second chance still under construction. It made her even more excited to finish the work at Grams'.

She glanced across the bar at Noah. He was quiet this morning, more than usual. Focused, but distracted. Something was on his mind, and Emily hoped by his expression that it wasn't their almost kiss.

Carly tested the newly wired jukebox. "I think these are mostly upbeat classics," she said cheerfully, tapping the screen.

The speakers crackled. Then a haunting guitar riff rolled out, slow and deliberate. "Brothers in Arms."

Noah froze.

Emily was the first to see it. The shift. The way Noah's hand, resting on the edge of the bar, curled into a fist. His spine too straight. His jaw too tight.

His voice, when it came, was barely audible. "Where'd that song come from?"

Carly blinked. "It was just on the playlist. Want me to skip it?"

Before she could reach the screen, something clattered. Someone behind the bar dropped a glass. It hit the tile with a sharp crack. Almost immediately, a truck backfired in the parking lot.

Noah flinched. Not dramatically, but enough. He turned and walked swiftly out the door. Carly followed.

Emily dropped the rag she'd been holding and went outside, too.

Carly was standing beside him near the edge of the porch, looking unsure of what to say. Emily approached quietly and placed her hand on Noah's arm. His muscles were rigid beneath the soft white cotton of his T-shirt.

He glanced over at Emily. His usually smiling face was a stony, empty mask.

"You okay?" she asked.

"Leave it alone, Emily," he said. He ran a frustrated hand through his hair and twisted away from the women. He turned to glance one more time at Emily, then jogged off toward his truck. Carly shook her head as he disappeared.

• • • •

NOAH WALKED FROM HIS truck to the houseboat on shaky legs, heart pounding in his head.

*Breathe in. Breathe out.*

He crossed the dock and the deck. He closed the sliding glass doors of the boat with more self-control than he thought he had. He was shaking. He had almost lost it in front of Carly. And Emily. Sadie did nervous circles around his legs as he bent over, hands on hips, gasping for breath.

*Breathe in. Breathe out.*

What would Emily have thought if he had really had a meltdown? How upset would Carly have been? He continued to hide the panic attacks from his sister. She didn't need to worry about him. She had enough to worry about. He should have known Kevin's' call would send him into a tailspin. As if the upcoming memorial for Benjamin wasn't enough.

*Breathe in. Breathe out.* His heartbeat was slowing, but not fast enough. He needed to run. He stripped off work clothes and threw them on the floor. He'd pick them up later. He needed to run now. Needed to exercise the tension out of his muscles. Needed to work out the adrenaline.

• • • •

EMILY WATCHED HIM DISAPPEAR around the corner before lowering herself into one of the rocking chairs on the porch. The drink she'd left on the bar no longer sounded appealing.

The door creaked open behind her a few minutes later. Daniel stepped out, her forgotten water bottle in hand. Wordlessly, he passed it to her and sat down beside her.

"He's been through a lot, hasn't he?" she asked, her gaze still fixed on the spot where Noah had disappeared.

"Yes, he has. And according to Carly, he doesn't talk about it much. And then Benjamin. I think it's all taking a toll on him that he doesn't let us see."

"My husband is an alcoholic. I've been wearing myself out taking care of him for two years. I'm not sure I have the energy to put into a relationship. Not one like Noah deserves."

"Not all men are like your husband, Emily. Noah takes care of Carly, and Carly takes care of him. Joey and Carly do the same."

"I've noticed that. Eddie and me always had problems. I think I knew from the beginning. I just kept trying because I thought that's what I was supposed to do. My grandparents had such a wonderful relationship. I kept trying to make mine and Eddie's relationship like that. The harder I tried, the worse it became."

"You can't force a relationship, Emily. It's either there or it isn't. And it takes two to make a relationship work. Or fail. It can work both ways."

"I haven't been single in almost a decade. And I'm still not. I know nothing about dating or relationships anymore," she said, twisting the ring she still wore. She didn't know anything about marriage either anymore.

"You wouldn't have to take care of Noah, you know. He's good at taking care of himself. I know he had it rough when he came back from Iraq the last time, but he pulled himself together. He didn't drown his miseries, blame someone else, or let himself sink into depression. He got up every morning and dealt with it. He still has scars, but he wears them well. As do you."

He wasn't referring to the scar on her face. He was talking about Eddie. Emily rocked slowly, taking a sip of her drink. "I like being with Noah."

Daniel nodded, "Well, that's a start."

"I think I'm going to head out. Will you say goodbye to the others for me?"

"Of course," he said. "Good luck."

• • • •

EMILY WALKED UP TO Noah's boat. She knocked on the door, but there was no answer. His truck was out front, so he must have gone for a run. She was still standing there by the boat, nervously shifting from one foot to the other, when he walked up. When he looked at her, his eyes were dark.

"Hi," she said.

"What are you doing here?" His voice was flat, like his eyes.

Unsure of herself, she said. "Maybe I should go."

She lowered her head and moved to walk around him.

A hand on her arm stopped her. She made no move to turn or say anything, simply stood there, waiting.

"Emily," he said softly. "Wait."

She turned slowly, eyes still not reaching his. He reached down and lifted her chin with a finger.

"I'm sorry," he said, his eyes filled with sadness. "About this morning. And about earlier. Why don't you stay for a bit? Have a drink with me."

"Are you sure?"

His lips curved into a slight smile. "Positive. I can't promise I'll be the best company, but I'll try."

"You want to help yourself?" he said, gesturing to the small bar after they walked in. "I'm gonna shower real quick."

Shower. That word brought up all kinds of mental pictures. Warm water, soap. She shook her head to clear her head and made herself at home and poured a drink. With a drink in hand, she went outside to sit in the deck chair. Sadie followed, looking up expectantly.

"I didn't bring your friend this time," she said, patting the dog's big head.

She was finishing the drink, staring out at the water when Noah came back out. The drink was more amber than dark. No beer today, apparently. He needed something stronger.

His hair was still wet from the shower and he was wearing jogging pants and an old red Marine t-shirt with the words "Semper Fi" blazing in yellow. He left the screen door open, and soft rock music drifted from the speakers.

Emily got up for a refill. When she got back, Noah had propped his feet up on the railing and was staring out at the water. Emily sat back and nervously chewed her lip. Should she try to talk to him? Should she sit there quietly? Should she leave?

"You don't have to stay here, Emily," he said.

*Does he want me to leave?*

"But I'd like it if you stayed," he finished.

Emily let out the breath she didn't even realize she'd been holding. "I'll stay for a little bit."

"I don't have as many melt-downs as I used to. I guess I should be thankful for that."

"Meltdowns?" she asked, sitting down.

"Yeah. When I got back from Iraq, my head was messed up. You see some stuff over there that you should never see. Especially when you're young and immature. It's pretty hard stuff to deal with. I started having anxiety attacks. They call it PTSD. Nightmares. I deal with them better these days, but certain things can trigger them. Crowds. I can't stand to feel like I'm stuck somewhere. Loud and unexpected noises."

"What do you do?"

"Most of the time, I just remove myself from the situation, or avoid things that might cause them. Crowds, for instance. I avoid drinking a lot. If I drink too much, I don't have as much control. Running helps. I guess it's the endorphins. My superior is coming for a visit, and while we're friends it's like a double edged sword. It brings back memories I've packed away."

"Daniel said you don't like to talk about it."

"I don't."

"We don't have to then. But we can if you want. And it doesn't have to be today."

He fell silent again, and Emily thought of Eddie. How would Eddie have dealt with the same problem? Alcohol. He would have drunk until he passed out. Or lashed out at someone, Emily. But Noah? He refrained from drinking, knowing it would make it worse. The contrast between the two men struck her again. What would a relationship be like with Noah? Not like the one she just left, that was for damn sure.

"What a fine pair we are." Noah said with a short laugh.

Emily grinned. "It would seem so."

"How about we take the boat out?" he said. "The dolphins should be coming in soon. And I need to move around."

Soon, they were out on the water, a few miles from the coast. Noah stopped the boat and dropped anchor. He refreshed his drink and rejoined her on the deck. He motioned for her to stand with him. As she stood beside him, she tried to keep from bumping into him as the boat rocked slightly.

He touched her arm lightly and pointed to a spot not far from them. A dark form jumped up out of the water, the fin mimicking the waves it was riding on.

Another dolphin joined the first one. The two met and did a twist together as they glided back into the water.

"Wow," Emily said. "That's so beautiful."

"They're mating."

Emily blushed, "Really?"

He grinned, "Yep."

She watched as the two dolphins continued to twist gracefully in and out of the water.

"Amazing." she said as a few more dolphins joined them.

Noah disappeared into the boat for a moment and turned the stereo off. The only sounds were the sounds of the sea birds overhead, and the waves softly slapping the sides of the boat. Emily watched the dolphins as they rose in and out of the waves, their grey bodies shining in the sun.

Emily scooted closer to Noah, nudging his arm as the dolphins continued their antics. Entranced by the animals, neither noticed the large boat that passed. The wake shook the boat and Emily stumbled slightly, falling against Noah. He reached an arm around her to steady her, pulling her against his chest.

She realized she was holding his arms. His muscles flexed under her palms. She pressed close to him, her body touching his. She looked up. His eyes locked on her mouth. She couldn't move. She knew he was going to kiss her. She was going to let him. And this time, there would be no interruptions.

Slowly, he lowered his mouth to hers. His lips moved slowly at first, a cautious exploration. Her lips opened for his, and the kiss deepened, became more aggressive. A hand roamed up her back to cradle her head. His fingers curled into her hair. Her hands moved up his arms to his neck.

The boat rocked again and jolted them. They steadied themselves by grabbing onto each other and regaining their footing. Noah's eyes burned into hers, and they were silent. He reached a hand up to her cheek and leaned down, placing a soft kiss on her forehead. Her heart thundered in her chest. Every nerve ending tingled.

A long second later, he looked down at her.

He smiled. "How about another drink? And are you hungry?"

Emily couldn't speak at first. Her lips still tingled, her brain still short-circuited.

But she managed a breathless, "Yes. To both."

"What would you like?"

She shook her head. "No clue. Have anything in mind?"

"I don't want to be around people yet," he said. "You want me to cook something?"

"You cooked the last time," she protested.

"How about we both cook," He suggested. "It'll keep my mind off things too."

Him. Her. Small kitchen. Not good. But she nodded anyway.

"You know," he said, I have some chicken and sausage we should do something with."

Emily's eyes lit up. "We could make a jambalaya."

"That, my dear Emily, sounds great. You tell me what you need."

She started rattling off a list of things they needed.

"Got it," he started pulling onions and bell peppers out of the small dorm sized refrigerator.

"Cutting board?" she asked.

He handed her a board and a knife.

She started slicing and dicing. So intent was she on the task that she didn't notice that Noah had fallen silent.

"What?" she asked when she saw his stare.

"I've never seen you like this."

"Like what?" she asked.

He paused, as if looking for the right word. "Passionate? Your face just lit up when I put that knife in your hand and you started."

"You make me sound like a serial killer," she said.

"You'd be a sexy serial killer," he said, and she blushed. "I'll have to have you over and cook with me more often. You make it so much more enjoyable."

She cut her eyes at him. "Behave."

"I am," he laughed. "Trust me. I am behaving."

She looked in his eyes, saw them darken. She knew he was thinking about that kiss earlier. Just like she was.

"Speaking of behaving," she said, changing the subject. "Remember when we got into trouble with Pops?"

"Which time?" he asked.

"The time he let us take the boat out, and we anchored and swam until we were so exhausted that we fell asleep."

"I remember that. He was livid," Noah said.

"And I was grounded for a month!" she said. "He almost wouldn't let us take the boat out again."

"Pops was a good man," Noah said. "I miss him. And Grams."

Emily looked down at the onions. "They were good people."

"Yes, they were."

Emily scraped the onions into a bowl and started on the bell peppers. "So, Noah, you never married?"

"Nope. Guess I just haven't found anyone to put up with me yet," he grabbed her empty glass and his own and went to refill them.

He handed her the glass. "You let me know what you need me to do. Want me to make a salad?"

"That would be great. I'll tell you when. This has to simmer for a while," she said. She put the remaining ingredients in the pan and adjusted the heat. "Now, all we do is wait."

"Awesome," he said. "How about we finish our drinks on the deck?"

"That's a great idea." His proximity was wearing her defenses thin. She grabbed her glass and followed him to the deck.

They talked quietly as the sun dipped lower over the water, the conversation easy and light for the first time all day. When Emily declared it ready, they went inside. Together, they spooned the food into mismatched bowls.

Once they were settled back outside with full plates and fresh drinks, Noah took a bite and groaned in appreciation.

"This is incredible," Noah said after taking a bite.

She smiled and took a sip of her drink. They spent the rest of the meal talking about the weather, the changes in the area since she left, and about Carly. They were simple and safe subjects. She caught herself yawning as he swept the plates away.

"Tired?" he asked.

"Actually, I am. I'll help you with the kitchen and head home,"

"I got the kitchen," he said. "I'll walk you home."

# Chapter Seventeen

*I*t was dusk. The sunlight glittered across the water like rubies, pink and shiny. Noah walked beside her. His hand was firm, holding hers. They walked along the beach until they reached a small point that formed a diamond. Noah sat down and gently tugged her down. She sank down beside him and crossed her legs Indian style, still keeping him at a distance. He ignored her imaginary line and scooted closer. Somehow, his nearness didn't bother her. She stretched her legs out in front, burying her toes in the cool sand. It was an invitation, and Noah accepted. He scooted closer, slid an arm around her shoulders. She scooted closer, too. His woodsy cologne mingled with the salty air. It was intoxicating. The sun continued setting; the moon was coming out, and a few stars were starting to dot the sky.

He leaned in closer to her; he was going to kiss her. Panicking, she turned away. Noah's face darkened, and he stood up. "Why are you afraid to be happy?"

Her mouth opened to answer, but the words never came.

He walked away.

Eddie was beside her now. "What? You think you deserve a man like that? He's way out of your league, sister." And he laughed. His laugh sounded like the shriek of a flock of seagulls.

• • • •

"EMILY, CAN YOU COME see me for a minute?" Carly shouted from the bar.

Emily wiped her hands on the towel in her back pocket. It was a habit she'd already picked up from Joey. She went through the swinging doors into the bar. Carly was hustling, arms filled with beer. The bar was loud and noisy, filled with bodies. Voices competed with Southern rock playing on the jukebox.

Snapper's was open, and the town had shown up like it was Mardi Gras.

Emily pushed through the kitchen doors and paused, heart swelling and stomach tightening all at once.

The place was packed.

Local fishermen had taken up one corner, swapping stories over buckets of beer. The fire station crew had dragged two tables together near the jukebox, already arguing about song picks and how to make the best spaghetti. Even the mayor of Bon Chance had come to show his support.

It was chaos. Emily could only imagine what tomorrow's grand opening and spaghetti cook off would be like.

Laughter spilled across the bar like spilled whiskey. There were handshakes and hugs, high fives and back claps. Carly moved behind the bar like a woman possessed. Pouring, swiping, answering questions three at a time.

This was more than opening day.

This was love. From the community. From every person who'd walked through the doors not only to grab a drink, but to be part of something.

"What do you need, Carly?" Emily asked.

"Text Noah, SOS. I need help."

"Got it!" Emily called back, pulling her phone from her pocket.

A familiar buzz hit her hand. She didn't think before answering.

"Hello?"

"Ms. Breaux? This is Chelsea with Jagneaux and Associates. I wanted to let you know that Mr. Breaux has been served the divorce papers."

"Oh..." Emily blinked. "Okay. Thank you."

She ended the call, but the words echoed through her mind like the dream she'd had that morning.

Eddie had been served the papers.

Emily's hands shook so badly she could barely type in the text to Noah. Luckily, Joey put her to work washing dishes. She would be useless with sharp objects until she got herself back together and her hands stopped shaking.

*This is what I wanted.* So why did it feel like a gut punch?

Soon, the back door to the kitchen opened, and Noah's tall form filled the doorway. Emily looked at him, before looking again at the sink. "You okay?"

She nodded, unwilling to speak. Afraid her voice would give her away.

"No, you aren't."

She nodded again.

"I'll be back. Let me see what Carly needs and I'll be back." He put a finger under her chin and pulled her face up gently. He looked into her eyes. "You got this. Whatever it is."

She smiled shakily and nodded again. He walked off, calling Carly's name.

• • • •

NOAH STEPPED INTO THE smoky bar and was hit with a wall of noise. Clinking glasses, laughter, boots scraping against the floorboards. Music pulsed from the jukebox like a second heartbeat. The air was thick, and his chest tightened before he even took a breath.

He scanned the crowd for Carly, trying to shove down the familiar hum of anxiety rising under his skin.

"Noah!" Carly waved from behind the bar. "Thank God you're here. Can you stock some beer in those spare coolers? We're running low."

"Sure thing," he said, forcing a grin that didn't quite make it to his eyes.

He grabbed the rolling coolers and started shoveling ice into them from the machine. The repetition helped. The scrape and crunch of ice. Nestling the beer in the ice.

He was almost finished with the second cooler when Carly called again.

"Noah!"

"What?" he yelled over his shoulder.

"There's someone here to see you."

He wiped his hands on a bar towel and turned.

His breath caught. Kevin Douglas.

The noise fell away. For a moment, it was just the beat of his pulse in his ears and the sudden, vivid memory of desert air and sand. His spine snapped straight, his body responding before his brain could.

*Not now. Not here.*

Still, he walked over and shook the man's hand, his grip firm even as anxiety coiled low in his gut.

"How are you?" Noah asked, voice tight.

"I'm good. Just got settled in over at the inn," Kevin replied. "Tried to call, but you weren't answering. Looks like you're busy. We can catch up later."

Noah nodded. "Yeah. I'll call you when I'm done here."

"Sounds good."

Noah gave him a nod and grabbed a bottle of Jack Daniels. He poured himself a shot and walked out through the kitchen, the nearest exit. He needed some air.

• • • •

EMILY DROPPED THE POT she was washing back into the water and lifted her head up, inhaling a deep breath. Noah was right. She could do this.

The call had shaken her more than she expected. She thought she'd be relieved. Instead, it felt like a quiet collapse inside her. A chapter ending with no confetti. No celebration.

The end.

The divorce was real now.

She blinked rapidly, willing her hands to stop trembling as she reached for the dish towel. Joey was still manning the grill, humming under his breath like nothing in the world could rattle him.

Emily dried the last pot and put it away.

"Hey, Joey?" she called.

"Yes?" he said, not even stopping to turn around.

"Need anything?"

"I'm good for now."

"I'm going outside for a minute. Get some fresh air."

"Gotcha. I'll yell if I need anything. Don't go far, though."

Emily escaped outside. She was glad there was a back entrance. She really didn't want to face anyone right now. She exhaled a shaky breath and leaned against the wall, closing her eyes.

The door opened quietly, and she heard footsteps on the wooden porch.

"Em, you okay?" It was Noah.

She started to nod, to reassure him that everything was okay, that she was just taking a break, but found herself shaking her head.

He enveloped her in his arms, and she rested her head on his shoulder.

He released his hold so he could look at her face. His palm touched her cheek. "You're going to be okay. Have a little faith in yourself, Em."

"I will, Noah."

"You will be fine. Trust me. We both will."

"You sure?" She looked up into his brown eyes, looking for reassurance. When her eyes met his, his eyes darkened. Emily chewed her bottom lip nervously, but found herself unable to look away. His other palm came up to touch her other cheek, framing her face.

"Positive," he said, lowering his mouth to hers.

Tiny shock waves of pleasure rolled through Emily's body as his lips made contact. Slowly, his lips glided over hers. His kiss was deliberate, reassuring, and an assault to her senses.

He retreated. His hands still caressing her face, he leaned down to kiss her forehead. "I'm here if you need me."

He enveloped her in another hug, then walked back into the bar.

Emily watched him walk away. She brought her fingers to her lips, remembering his kiss.

*Whiskey.*

There had been whiskey on his breath.

• • • •

THE BAR WAS QUIET.

Emily let out a slow breath, the tension finally easing from her shoulders. Her fingers curled around the cool glass of her beer, condensation dampening her palm. She sat at the bar, legs just brushing Noah's as he sipped slowly from a tumbler beside her.

Carly had switched off the jukebox and queued up one of her playlists. Something softer, swampy blues with a little soul. A gentle guitar twanged through the speakers, low and soothing. The lights were dimmed, casting golden pools across the scarred wood floors. Snapper's looked like it had exhaled.

Joey leaned back with a beer on the counter, one boot propped on a barstool rung. Carly was beside him.

"That was a hell of a day," Carly said.

"I'm just glad nobody set anything on fire," Noah added, raising his glass slightly toward Joey.

"Carly was too busy to be in the kitchen." Joey grinned.

Emily smiled, though her chest felt tight. The words from earlier still echoed in her head. She rubbed the condensation from her bottle and took a breath.

"They served him," she said softly.

The room stilled.

"Eddie?" Carly asked.

Emily nodded. "Got the call earlier. The papers were delivered."

Joey let out a slow breath, and Carly reached out to squeeze Emily's hand.

She looked over at Noah.

He held her gaze for a moment before setting down his glass.

"So that's what had you rattled earlier," he said. "The call."

Emily nodded.

"I know I'm the one who filed," Emily said, her voice tight. "I wanted this. I needed this. But it still feels..."

"Like an ending," Carly said quietly.

Emily nodded.

Noah leaned in closer. "You didn't end something," he said. "You made space for something new."

Carly raised her drink. "To endings."

Joey lifted his beer. "And beginnings."

Emily clinked her glass against theirs. "And friends."

The day had been exhausting physically, mentally, and emotionally. She fought back a yawn. She drained the rest of the bottle and scooted it to the front of the bar.

"Another one?" Carly asked.

"I'm good. I'm heading home. It's been a long day," Emily said, standing with a stretch.

"I'll walk you to your car," Noah said, already standing to join her.

"Oooh, don't do anything I wouldn't do," Carly called out.

Outside, the night wrapped around them. Warm, soft, a little electric. The parking lot was quiet except for the rhythmic chirp of crickets and the low thump of bass sneaking through the bar walls.

At her car, Emily turned toward him. "Thanks for... everything today."

Before she could say more, Noah stepped closer. "You've had a hell of a day, Em."

His hand brushed her cheek, and her breath caught. Then he kissed her. Really kissed her.

There was nothing tentative about it. His hands slid to her waist, drawing her in. Her fingers curled into his shirt, anchoring herself as the world narrowed to the taste of him. Whiskey and warmth, and a little wild. She melted into him, heart thudding, lips parting beneath his.

When he finally pulled back, his forehead rested against hers. His voice was rough.

"Tell me that didn't mess with your cook off game tomorrow."

She let out a breathless laugh. "I make a mean spaghetti sauce. Just so you know, I'll be the one in first place."

Noah grinned, opened her car door for her, and winked. "We'll see about that."

# Chapter Eighteen

Oscar whined, waking Emily up. She looked over to see his big head resting on the bed. Emily groaned and stretched. She padded through the house and let him out the door. He had finally calmed down enough to let him go without a leash. This place was good for him too. Yawning, she set the coffee pot, then went outside.

She propped bare feet up on the wooden porch railing. Leaning back on the Adirondack chair, she gazed up at the sky. The morning air was crisp. The air was cool on her bare toes and smelled of saltwater. She might light a fire in the fire pit later that night, if she felt like moving that much. She would have to see how the day played out.

Emily was restless. After all that had happened with Noah. Those kisses. And the notification that Eddie had received the divorce papers? It was a lot to process.

Emily thought of the flowerbeds at Grams'. There were still more weeds than there were plants or flowers. She checked on Oscar, who was still carousing in the surf. Maybe she'd pull a few weeds this morning. It was so early; she still had plenty of time before she had to get ready to go to Snapper's. She'd work off some nervous energy, so maybe she could focus.

Decision made, she rounded up Oscar in her car. When she got there, she secured his leash around a post on the porch. She trusted him on the beach, but not where there were roads. Then Emily brushed the hair out of her eyes and started pulling at weeds. Some of the droopy, fading plants in the flower beds around the house were salvageable. Like Emily, most just needed some TLC. She needed to pull the weeds that kept the flowers underneath from blooming. The remaining flowers and plants needed a good watering and feeding.

The sun was warm on her face. Maybe she'd tan a little more. She was still pale, pasty white like a vampire after months of nothing but work. They could cast her in that Passionflix Brotherhood vampire show she kept seeing social media posts about. She could use a little color in more ways than one. Her life had been black and white and lifeless for too long.

*Damn him.*

*Damn him for giving up and drowning in a bottle.*

*Damn him for trying to drown her too.*

How could he just sit there and do nothing? How could he choose a bottle over their relationship? Over her? And then scream at her like it was her fault?

She stood and kicked at a clump of dirt, sending it flying across the yard.

How fitting. That's what her life had done. Just crumbled.

She kicked another clump.

"Dumbass."

How could he let her feel like that? That the whole thing was her fault? Actually, she was the dumbass for putting up with it for so long.

"Asshole." She pulled out another clump of weeds.

So much for better or worse. She'd had the worse. It was time to find the better. And that better was Noah.

She threw another clump of weeds. Then she straightened up again. Putting her hands on her hips, she took a deep breath. She relished the feel of the blood coursing through her veins and the sun's warmth on her face. She felt strong, like an Amazon. She smiled.

"Feel better?"

She jumped slightly, startled. She turned to see Noah holding a thermos and two coffee cups.

"What are you doing?" she asked, a little more sharply than she intended to. Her embarrassment adding an edge to her voice.

His eyes sparkled despite the bags that were still underneath them. His lips twitched. He was about to laugh.

"Don't you dare laugh," Emily warned.

He bit his lip. "I wouldn't dare laugh at anyone carrying garden shears and throwing weeds like a wild woman."

She fought her own smile as he held out a cup. "Coffee, huh?"

She sighed, "Would love it. Come have a seat," she said, motioning to the porch swing.

As they walked up the stairs, she surveyed her progress in the flower beds. It was amazing what a little care and attention could do. Although the flowerbeds hadn't looked bad before, they hadn't looked good either. Now, all the stray weeds were gone. She had weeded out the junk. Left the strong plants. Plants that would continue to grow and even flower, eventually.

Emily wondered if she would look like that when all her weeds were gone. When there was nothing left to suck the life out of her. Even after a sleepless night, her eyes looked brighter now that they weren't red and bloodshot from exhaustion. She was still pale, but perking up. She was dealing with Eddie. Soon, he'd be no more than an unhappy memory. For now, she would just concentrate on the cook-off today.

"You okay?" Noah asked.

"Are you?" she countered. She wiped the dirt off her hands and smiled. Emily knew something was bothering him and was glad he hadn't pushed her away again.

"Yeah. Yeah, actually, I think I am," he said.

"It looks like we're both okay. Let me go wash up, and I'll have that cup of coffee. I'm going to need all the caffeine I can get to make it through today. And beat your behind at the cook off."

· · · ·

*JUST STARE AHEAD. NOAH told himself, looking at Benjamin's coffin. Just don't look. Don't look at the coffin. Noah's thoughts drowned out the priest's voice as he went through the last part of the funeral service.*

*His parents sat in the chairs in front of him. His mother sobbed quietly into a handkerchief. Carly sat beside her. Carly stared at the coffin, clutching Joey's dress pants. Her knuckles were white against the black fabric.*

*Don't look. Don't look at the coffin.*

*Daniel stood off to the side with Glinda. She held a handkerchief to her nose. Sunglasses shielded her eyes. Daniel patted her hand as it rested in the crook of his arm. A cool breeze blew through the small, green tent, blowing the black veil on the hat that adorned Glinda's head. Emily stood a step behind Daniel, on the edge of the crowd. Noah was envious. He could handle the edge. He wanted to be on the edge.*

*Despite the crisp air, Noah's face flushed. He longed to pull the tie away from his throat. Air, he needed more air. He was suffocating.*

Don't look.

*Standing on the other side were Gabriel, Grace, and Ryder. The two guys flanked Grace as always, a protective barrier. Gabe shifted as if uncomfortable in something other than a t-shirt and jeans. Grace, who always wore black, looked pale and oddly frail in the somber dark dress. Ryder wore a black cowboy hat and jeans. He looked like he always did, but his devil-may-care smile was missing.*

*Noah's face grew hotter. His heartbeat pounded in his ears. His eyes darted to the corners of the tent. There was no leaving. Not now. He was trapped. The open green tent was a cage.*

*More pressure in his head. He was going to blow. More pounding. He took an unconscious step backward, wincing when he backed into the mourner behind him. Trapped.*

*His eyes caught movement by the coffin. The priest was clasping his mother's hand. It was over. He took a shuddering breath. The crowd behind him shifted as the mourners made a line to pay their final respects to the family.*

*Noah turned on the ball of his foot. Resisting the urge to run, he walked swiftly away.*

...

Noah shook the memory off and turned his attention to Carly, who had taken her place on the makeshift porch they had made on Snapper's porch. Folding chairs were lined in the parking area in front. A large picture of Benjamin proudly displaying a good day's catch was on an easel near where Carly was standing.

Carly took the mic. "I want to thank you all for coming out today. I wanted to do this before everything got all crazy with the cook off."

She stopped a moment and looked down at the ground before continuing, "Benjamin lived to fish. Every spare moment he had, he had a fishing pole in his hand."

She gestured to the building behind her. "This was one of his favorite places in town. Every fishing trip he took started here."

"Ben was the smallest of our group," Carly continued. "But, what he lacked in size, he made up for in wit. He'd snap right back with a comeback that would cut you damn near to the bone. He earned that nickname Snapper, like a snapping turtle."

Someone came to stand next to him. It was Emily. She reached out for his hand and whispered. "Sorry I'm late."

He squeezed her hand in response.

Carly smiled. "In a few minutes, our teams will begin setting up for the cook off. Our family wants to thank you for coming. All proceeds will go to create a scholarship in Ben's name."

Joey handed her a bottle of Ben's favorite beer. Taking it in hand, she said, "We thought about doing a ribbon cutting ceremony, but that didn't really fit Ben. So we thought we'd christen this place like a boat."

Joey held out a big black trash can, and Carly took the bottle and slammed it into the porch railing.

Nothing happened.

Carly slammed it again, harder this time.

Still nothing.

Carly looked up and grinned at the crowd. She popped the top on the beer and took a big swig.

"Ben never did like to see a good beer go to waste." She said, sending the crowd into laughter.

She poured some of the beer on the ground. "To Ben!"

"To Ben!" the crowd called.

"Please stay and enjoy this beautiful day and some wonderful spaghetti."

As Carly stepped down from the porch, the crowd milled about, some to say hello to the family, some to walk into the bar to check out the changes.

As the crowd dispersed, Emily leaned into Noah's side for a moment. "I need to go grab my stuff from the car. It took me longer to pack up than I thought it would."

He nodded. "Want help?"

She shook her head. "I've got it."

Noah watched her walk away, sunlight catching on the edges of her brown hair. The sound of portable tables and tents being erected filled the air. Noah exhaled. The hardest part of the day, the memorial, was over.

• • • •

EMILY GRABBED THE REST of the plastic shopping bags from the back of the SUV. Hopefully, she had remembered everything. It felt so weird cooking outside of a kitchen or outside in general. Other than to grill, she'd never cooked outside before. This was definitely another new experience. Luckily, Noah had an extra burner to use. Carly was using an electric one inside to monitor the bar. Apparently, they were expecting a crowd for today's event. It would be an even bigger crowd than yesterday. *Nice, an audience.*

Noah waved her over to the spot where he was set up in the parking lot in front of the bar.

"Hey," she said.

Noah had already set up two tables and two propane tanks with burners. Usually, it was the setup used for crawfish boils. Emily chewed her bottom lip nervously. Seeing her hands full of the shopping bags, Noah reached out to help.

"I'll help you out as much as I can with the burner," Noah said. "I can't help with the actual cooking, though. I want to win fair and square."

The cooking she could do. Setting the rest of the bags on the tables, she started sorting vegetables, cans of tomato sauce and tomato paste, and spices. When finished, she looked around. To her left, Joey had a table and a burner and was already slicing and dicing.

*Overachiever.*

Red and Walter, two locals, had two tables together. They had decided to cook as well. But they hadn't started yet. Their bags were still on the table. They had chosen to take a break and were sitting in their folding chairs drinking beer, their long legs stretched out.

Jay, a friend of Carly's, had the same idea. Bags were out on his table, and he had joined Red and Walter by their tables and burners for a beer and some pre-cook-off trash talk.

Joey was already working. His station was set up and pristine. He would do some cutting, then some cleaning.

Other tables were set up, but Emily didn't know any of those people. Some were locals, and some were representatives from various oil companies, judging from the logos on their tents. Taking a cue from Joey and Noah, Emily chopped onions to get the sauce started.

Music filtered out from the open bar doors. It was a nice accompaniment to the light conversation and dock noise. It was a weekend, and boats were going in and out of the water. Some for fishing, some out to enjoy the water and sunshine. A light breeze blew, keeping things cool. It would be chilly when the sun went down, but everyone would be done by then.

"You ready for the burner?" Noah asked her.

"Yes," she said, glancing down at the pile of onions.

"I'll take care of that," he said. Emily watched as he lit the burner and adjusted the flame.

"That's good?" he asked.

She nodded, "It'll do."

He smiled at her. "Let me know, and I can make it hotter for you."

The gleam in his eyes made it clear he wasn't talking about just the flame coming from the propane tank. She swallowed hard and nodded.

Carly approached with plastic cups in hand. "Mimosas, anyone?"

"I'd love one," Emily said.

Carly handed her a glass and laughed when Noah turned his nose up when she tried to give him one.

"Not for you?" she asked.

"Um, no. Too sweet."

Carly took a sip of hers and took a seat in the extra chair Noah had set out. She watched as Emily and Noah periodically got up to add a spice or stir their sauces.

"You still cooking, Carly?" Emily asked.

"Yep. Doesn't take me long. Call me 'Carly Boyardee.'"

"You're not really making your spaghetti from a can, are you?" Emily looked at her, aghast.

"No. Not really. The noodles aren't in a can," Carly said.

"I told you, Carly can't boil water," Noah said.

"It's true," Carly said. "Cooking isn't my thing. I put together an excellent salad to go with the spaghetti and bought garlic bread. That, I can do."

Joey had finished the prep work and was now stirring the sauce. His face was serious, dimples gone. Unlike the others, he didn't take part in the teasing comments about who would win. Red, Walter, and Jay were still taking a break. Emily glanced at her watch. They still had a couple of hours before judging. Some people liked to wait until the last minute, she guessed. Or some were there to have a good time and not taking their cooking too seriously.

"Well, I'm going to go see what everyone else is up to," Carly said, jumping up. "Time to socialize. My favorite part," she said with a wink.

Emily shook her head as Carly walked away. "She's something else."

"Yes, she is," Noah agreed. "How's your fire going? Need me to turn it up?"

Images of that last kiss popped in her mind. Yes, yes I do, she thought. She glanced at the fire burning under the saucepot. "I think I'm okay." She paused for a moment, then raised an eyebrow. "For now."

He winked, which sent delicious shivers down her spine. "Just let me know."

"I will."

Emily watched as the three guys across from them grabbed another beer and prepared their ingredients. It was time to get serious and get down to business. Well, as serious as they got, she thought. Emily noticed that instead of cutting their own vegetables, they had bought the pre-chopped version. Emily grinned. She guessed that was one way to do it. It saved cooking time and added to drinking time.

Everything in the pot, Emily relaxed into the folding chair Noah had brought. She was lounging in the sun, sunglasses on.

She heard someone walk up and opened her eyes to see Ryder's grin. She smiled back.

"I came by to let you know Carly asked me to judge today."

"Is that right?" Emily asked.

"Yep. And to let you know my vote can be bought," he flashed his dimples.

"Oh, really?" Emily looked at Noah. "And are you making that same offer to ALL contestants?"

Ryder laughed, "Nope. My services are only for the female contestants."

Emily shook her head, "No, as tempting as your offer is...," she laughed. "I will win fair and square. No judge tampering."

"I tried," he tipped his black cowboy hat, "I'll see you later."

Emily took a moment to taste the spaghetti sauce. She needed more garlic, but had diced all that she had brought with her.

"I need some more garlic," she said. "I'm going to run over to the house and get some more. I can do that, right?"

"I don't see why not," Noah responded.

"I'll be right back," Emily said and left. As she walked to her car, her phone vibrated. It was Eddie's sister. She put the phone back in her pocket. Whatever his sister wanted could wait. It was probably about the divorce and she had no desire to hash that out with her. She was not going to let Eddie or his family ruin her day today.

· · · ·

NOAH WATCHED EMILY walk off, his gaze lingering longer than he meant it to. There was something about the way she moved, like she was finally settling into herself again. He exhaled, reaching for his drink, just as someone stepped up beside him.

"Gorgeous day today," Kevin said, nodding toward the water.

"Yeah," Noah replied. The initial shock of Kevin's visit had worn off and Noah was becoming more comfortable. There were bad memories, but good ones as well. Carousing in bars around the world, playing cards in the barracks, and other shenanigans only enlisted men could get themselves into.

They stood in companionable silence for a beat, watching the bustle of prep and chatter around the makeshift cooking stations. Music and laughter spilled from the open doors of the bar.

"Smells good already," Kevin added. "If I'd known the whole town would turn out, I might've entered too."

Noah shot him a sidelong look. "Didn't know you could cook."

Kevin grinned. "I can't. But I can supervise like a pro."

Noah laughed. "Carly already has that job covered."

A car Noah didn't recognize pulled into the lot. The passenger door flung open, and a man stumbled out, unsteady on his feet. A woman got out slower, her expression taut with unease. The man was wobbly. He'd either started early or was still drunk from the night before. This was not a good sign. The drunken man walked up to the tables where Joey and Noah were. Noah exchanged a look with Joey, and they stood up.

"Where is she?" the man demanded. He was obviously inebriated. The word she came out like a hiss. Sheeeeee. His face was red and swollen from too much alcohol in his body for too long. He swayed slightly, and with that rounded belly, reminded Noah of one of those Weeble Wobble toys he'd played with as a child. Stains spotted his already dirty shirt, and he reeked of stale beer. *Eddie,* Noah thought, his blood began to boil.

Joey, always the diplomat, was the one to try to reason with Eddie. "Sir, who are you talking about?"

The inebriated man turned to Joey. "My wife. Emily Breaux. Not that it's any of your busssinessssss."

"Actually, this is my bar, so it is MY business. I would appreciate it if you would calm down."

"I'm not calming down until you tell that selfish bitch to get her ass out here. And while you're at it, tell that sonofabitch she's sleeping with to get out here too. He said his name was Ryder. R-y-d-e-r." He mimicked the way Ryder had spelled his name that day on the phone.

"Eddie!" the woman with him gasped. She came up behind him and grabbed his arm to pull him away. Eddie shook her off.

Noah felt the muscle in his cheek twitch, but said nothing. He looked at Joey, who had lost his patience at "bitch." He could also feel the chill in the atmosphere around. Emily was a woman, and in this community, respect was a given. Especially to one of their own. This could get ugly quick. And he involved Ryder, who had no patience and been in more than one bar fight. He stepped around the cooking table and took a step closer to Eddie. This was not good, because he didn't need to be within grabbing distance of the guy, either.

"Well, are you going to tell me where ssshe is?" Eddie bellowed.

Noah was close enough to smell the alcohol on Eddie's breath. He flinched, but kept his eyes on Eddie. He concentrated on keeping his hands at his sides as the debilitating moves he'd learned in training flashed through his mind.

"Sir, I don't know who you're talking about. If you calm down, we can talk about it." Joey attempted to calm him again.

"You know who I'm talking about. I know she's here. That slut. I shoulda known she wouldn't wait long."

Noah took another step forward. Sweat popped out on his forehead. He was dangerously close to losing it. Out of the corner of his eye, he saw Kevin step up and stand beside him.

"Devereaux," he said, his voice low.

Noah cut his eyes over at Douglas. Douglas shook his head.

"Okay, sir. I'm going to have to ask you to leave," Joey said again.

"I'm not leaving until you tell me where she is," he turned to face Joey, wobbling slightly.

Noah exhaled a deep breath. His hands itched. He wanted to get his hands on this guy. He looked at Kevin again.

"No."

Noah heard movement on the rocky parking lot and on the bar's wooden porch. They had attracted attention from the bar. Yep, this was going to get ugly.

"Sir, you can see she's not here. You need to go," Joey said.

Eddie slowly glanced around the bar. "She's with that guy, isn't she? Where is HE? Wait til I get my handssss on him. Is he scared or something?"

Ryder stepped out into the circle. "Scared of you? I don't think so. You were looking for me?" He took a long sip from a beer bottle and sat it on the porch railing. He pulled a cigarette out of the pack and lit it, eyes never leaving Eddie.

"Kevin?" Noah asked. His voice was a growl.

"Sir, I'm going to ask you one more time to leave. Don't make me call the cops," Joey said.

"And I'm telling you one more time I'm not. Not without her. Where is she?" He took a wobbly step toward Ryder.

"It's you! "He took another step and Noah stepped in his way. Ryder wasn't far behind.

"Move," Eddie said. "This is between me and him."

Noah's fists flexed. "Now it's between you and me."

Noah was seconds away from lunging when he heard Emily. She stood just behind Eddie.

"Eddie," she said. Her face was pale.

Eddie turned, wobbling slightly still.

"Leave Eddie," Emily said.

"I'm not leaving without you, Emily."

"I'm not going, Eddie. Leave." Emily walked around to stand by Noah, facing Eddie.

"You're going. You don't get to just leave." Eddie reached out to grab her arm. Emily jerked away and stepped back.

Eddie, reaching out and grabbing nothing, lost his balance and stumbled forward. He slammed into Emily and she hit the table. The table and Emily went flying backwards. Noah tried to catch her, but it was too late. Like a set of dominoes, Eddie fell, Emily fell, the table fell, and the table knocked the pots and burners over. Dark red sauce leaked out on the gray rocks of the parking lot.

Noah watched Emily's face crumple.

He reacted. Not one to hit a man while he was down, Noah grabbed Eddie by the collar and hoisted him to his feet. When Eddie was standing, he looked him in the eye. With one hand, he held Eddie's collar. His other hand clenched into a fist. Resisting the urge to punch, he reared back his hand and backhanded Eddie across the face.

"That's for Emily," he said as Eddie fell to the ground.

Noah looked at Emily, who stood there speechless. Carly, Daniel, and Kevin were standing there with her. Noah could see her lip quiver.

"Noah, help me out with this. Let's get him back in the car," Joey said.

"I'm not touching him again," Noah said. "Let the bastard lie there."

"Wait!" Emily said. Noah looked at her. Her chest was heaving. "He wants to see me? Well, here I am."

• • • •

EMILY WALKED OVER AND looked down at Eddie. Her hands shook, her head pounded like a drum.

"How could you do this to me? I worked two jobs for you. *Two!*" Her voice cracked through the quiet. Noah, Joey,

Ryder, and Kevin stepped closer, forming a silent wall behind her. Carly raised her glass in a slow, satisfied salute.

"Get 'em, girl," she mouthed.

"I gave up everything for you. My dream of opening a restaurant drowned right alongside your sorrows. You lost your job. You can't find another one. And somehow, that's *my* fault?"

She ran a trembling hand through her hair. "For better or worse, my ass. There hasn't been a *better* in years."

She reached into her pocket and pulled out the ring. The symbol of everything they once promised. Everything he broke. It was like an albatross around her neck.

"I should've thrown this in the gulf the day I left," she said. "But I guess I needed to see your face one last time."

She tossed the ring onto his stomach. It bounced off and skittered into the gravel with a sharp metallic *clink*.

"I'm done with that. I'm done with you."

She looked him in the eye, voice steady. "You make me sick."

And then she turned and walked away.

* * * *

EMILY WALKED DOWN THE beach, away from Eddie, away from the disgusting things he said, away from the image of her sauce, red and ruined on the ground. She still shook with fury. Throwing the ring at him had not been enough. She wished she could've ground the ring into the ground and sprinkled him with the dust, like ashes. Heart pounding and chest heaving, she stared out at the water. She turned when she heard footsteps approaching. She turned and faced the water again when she saw it was Noah.

"Emily?" His voice was soft. "He's gone. Kevin and Joey loaded him into the car. I guess that was his sister?"

Emily nodded.

"She apologized for him. Said she tried to call when she realized how bad off he was. She only brought him because she was afraid he would drive and kill someone."

She turned. "How could he do this, Noah?"

"I don't know."

She said, "I'm moving into Grams' as soon as possible."

"It's about damn time," he said finally.

"Will you help me?"

"Absolutely."

She reached up, put her hands on each side of his face, and planted a kiss firmly on his lips. She grinned as his eyes widened in shock. "Let's go get a drink. I think I want to celebrate."

"Hold on just one second," he said.

"What?"

He smiled and pulled her in close so that their bodies were touching. The heat of his body against hers drove out all thoughts of celebrating, of the cook off, of Eddie. When his lips met hers, shock waves pulsed through her body. She let all her defenses drop and kissed him back without reserve. Her hands trailed across his back, reveling in the feel of him.

Finally, breathless, he pulled back. "If we're going to go back to the cook-off, we better go now."

Emily took a deep, steadying breath. "Then we better go," she said, brushing a kiss to his jaw. "But your sauce isn't the only thing simmering."

• • • •

THEY WERE WALKING ARM in arm when they returned to the parking lot. Noah frowned as he saw a Pointe Shade patrol car pull into the parking lot.

"What now?" Noah asked.

They went to stand beside Kevin, who nodded.

"Are we having a little problem here?" Officer Mouton asked, walking up. His eyes scanned the crowd.

"No problems here, officer," Noah said.

"Heard there was a minor altercation here a few minutes ago," Mouton said, his thumbs tucked in the belt buckle.

"As you can see, there's absolutely nothing going on but a spaghetti cook-off," Noah said.

"Well, I'd like to speak to the owner. And your sister as well."

"Actually, I own as much of this bar as Carly does, and I say there's not a problem. And I think you're out of your jurisdiction. Am I right?"

"Well, you know. Just doing my civic duty."

"Sure you are."

"If you're sure," Mouton said. "I'll be leaving then. Tell Carly that I'll be seeing her." He tipped his officer's hat and walked away.

"What was that all about?" Kevin asked as the cop drove away.

"Long story. But I don't think it's going to have a happy ending."

"Maybe it's time for some changes in La Fleur Parish." Kevin said. "I am considering a change in employment."

"You, my friend," Noah said, "would be the perfect man to take on that job."

Kevin threw an arm around Noah's shoulder. "We'll see. For now, we could all use a drink."

•  •  •  •

THE SCENT OF GARLIC and tomato still hung in the air, mingling with the breeze drifting in from the gulf. A few stragglers milled around, plastic cups in hand, their laughter mingling with the music from the D.J..

"You okay?" Carly asked Emily.

"Actually, I'm better than I've been in a long time," she responded.

"Sounds like something that deserves a toast," Carly said. "Mimosa?"

"Would love one."

Emily looked over to where her table had been. The table was upright. Wet rocks replaced the red mess the sauce made. The burner had been put back together, and she could see a pot bubbling on it.

Emily looked at Carly. "What's up with that?"

"Everyone got together and whipped up another sauce for you. Joey, Red, Walter, and Jay all contributed something. Everybody but me, of course. I'm sure you didn't want any of my sauce. You can tweak it however you like and we'll consider it your entry and cooked by you."

Emily's eyes misted. "I don't know what to say."

"You don't have to say anything. We weren't going to let that drunken fool ruin your day," Daniel said as he walked up to Emily. Emily had forgotten he was also one of the judges. Glinda was with him.

Emily grinned. "Thank you guys so much. But, there goes my plan of celebrating and drinking. Now, I have to concentrate on this sauce."

"Honey," Carly said, laughing and pouring another mimosa. "I'll make sure you do both! Here's to you, Emily, here's to you."

While she sipped, Emily doctored the sauce the best she could. Judging time was quickly approaching. It wasn't her sauce, but it would work. She set up some serving bowls as Carly had instructed and readied the spaghetti for the judges. Daniel winked as he went to the judges' table. He wouldn't know which one was hers, but it felt good to have his support.

Jay, who had passed out on a table an hour ago, had roused long enough to cook the pasta and get his entry together. Red, Walter, and Joey were also getting their entries ready. Soon, Carly was scooping up the small bowls and bringing them to the judging area. Emily followed Noah into the bar to wait to hear the results. Jay and Walter were busy taunting each other.

Carly took the microphone from the D.J. "If I could have your attention, please. Before I announce the winners, I'd like to take a moment to thank everyone for coming out. Thank you for coming out to support a good cause and to honor the memory of a great man."

Carly held out a picture frame. "This is the last picture we all took together. A summer many years ago. More than I care to admit," she said, and laughter filled the bar. "I'm going to put this picture up here in the bar, to remind us that nothing is more important than our friends and family. And to always remember the good times."

Carly's smile faltered for a moment. "Speaking of good times. Let's announce the winners of the first annual Benjamin Devereaux Memorial Cook-Off. "In third place, it's Jay Thibodaux."

"In second, it's Walter Boudreaux," the crowd cheered.

"And in first place, it's Joey Delchamp."

"How did Jay beat me?" Red asked. "He slept the last hour!"

Jay laughed, "I'm just good like dat."

Noah hugged Emily to him. "Upset that you didn't win?"

"Nah," she said. "I won more today than a cook-off."

Holding his beer out, toasted, "You did, my dear. Yes, you did."

# Chapter Nineteen

A rms full of grocery bags, Emily bumped the door closed with her hip. Other than the happy taps of Oscar's feet on the laminate floor, the house was quiet. After the chaos of the last few days, it was welcome. Weird, but welcome.

When Noah had promised to get her into Grams' house, now her home, he'd meant it. He'd summoned the troops, so to speak, and everyone had reported for duty. Carly helped her clean and move her things from the cabin. Joey assisted Noah with repairs. Glinda and Daniel kept them all fueled with food and coffee. Even Kevin Douglas had shown up to pitch in. There was still some minor work to be done, but it was enough to get her moved in.

She put the last of the groceries away and poured a glass of wine and leaned against the now gleaming counter. The curtains waved in rhythm with the ceiling fan, and Emily smiled. She would keep the curtains for now. Along with other items that reminded her of Grams.

It was her first night in her new home. *Her* home. Not her and her husband's, not a temporary cabin. But something permanent.

She sighed. New home. New life. Now what?

The question lingered in her mind. She had some money left over from Grams', after the repairs and attorney fees. Eddie wasn't pursuing a long, drawn out divorce, much to her surprise. Her lawyer had called after the cook off and said that Eddie was agreeing to the divorce. He even declined to take his share of her savings. Emily didn't know why, but she was grateful. And even more excited to get on with her new life.

Her phone vibrated on the counter. It was Noah.

**Noah:** How are you liking the house?

**Emily:** Loving it.

**Noah:** Too quiet for you?

Emily thought for a moment, before replying.

**Emily:** Maybe just a little.

**Noah:** Company?

They hadn't had any alone time since that kiss on the beach.

**Emily:** I would love some.

**Noah:** Be there in ten.

Smiling at the possibility of snuggling up to Noah on the porch swing with no interruptions this time, she put the phone down and went to freshen up—already wondering if she should offer him wine or... something stronger.

• • • •

NOAH WALKED UP ON EMILY'S porch, six-pack in hand. He wondered if he should have grabbed a pizza or something. He was so out of practice with this dating thing. Dating thing? Is that where they were? He thought of that last kiss on the beach. He didn't know if that's exactly what he would call it, but whatever it was; he liked it.

Emily opened the door as he started to knock. She was unbelievably sexy in her leggings and her hair in a messy bun. He longed to reach out and touch her hair, but that would probably need to wait for at least a "hello".

"Come on in." She opened the door and motioned him inside. "No Sadie tonight?"

"Nah, she looked too comfortable in her bed."

"Oscar will be disappointed."

He leaned down and patted the dog's head. "Next time, buddy."

She gestured to the glass of wine on the coffee table. "I have wine if you like. But it looks like you're good. Want me to put that in the fridge?"

"I got it."

"I thought we might sit outside on the porch for a bit. The weather is beautiful tonight for this time of year."

"That sounds perfect. I'll meet you out there."

Emily was curled in the corner of the porch swing, nestled against one of the colorful pillows Glinda had brought over to brighten up the place. The ceiling fan spun lazily overhead, stirring the scent of smoke from a neighbor's fire.

Beer in hand, he took a seat beside her. He reached out and put his arm around her shoulder. When she leaned in, he placed a kiss on the top of her head. Oscar curled up on the welcome mat, giving them a lazy side-eye of approval.

For a few moments, they sat in silence, listening to the soft creak of the swing and the quiet hum of night insects. Emily tucked her bare feet under her and took a sip of wine.

"Feels like Grams is still here somehow," she said softly, eyes scanning the porch rails, the potted ferns, and the wind chime that hadn't stopped since she got home.

"She'd be proud of you. This place already feels like yours." Noah took a sip of his beer.

"Everyone did such a great job. It means more than I can say."

They swung gently for a beat.

"So...what's next?"

Emily tilted her head. "Next as in tomorrow? Or next as in life?"

"You pick."

She let out a breath and looked out into the darkness. "Honestly? I don't know. For the first time in a long time, I don't have a plan. It's equal parts terrifying and kind of freeing."

He understood. It was how he had felt after leaving the Marine Corps. The freedom was exciting, but leaving behind the routines and structure had been hard. He understood why so many of his friends had re-enlisted.

"You'll find your way, Emily. It will just take some time. You said that you wanted to open your own place someday. Why not now?"

Another pause. This time, she fidgeted with a frayed edge on a pillow. "It's such a commitment and an expense. Rent, supplies, equipment..."

"What about that food truck or catering company? I said before that we need one of those here. We have more and more events."

"It's such an investment."

"Emily, are you trying to talk yourself out of this before you even start? Where there's a will, there's a way." he paused for a moment. "Hey, what about that cook-off? The one we got the information on in New Orleans?"

She grabbed her phone from the small table beside the swing. "I don't even know when it is. Let's see." She exhaled a sigh. "It's in two weeks. How will I ever be ready? That's a long shot."

"What do you have to lose? If nothing else, it will be great exposure and networking."

"You might be right. I need some help. I'll need taste testers."

"Oh, I'm sure we can find those for you."

"I need to feed you all anyway for helping me."

"Sounds like a plan. You round up some recipes, and I'll rally the troops. Again. You tell me when."

She hesitated, her fingers brushing his arm lingering just a second too long. The air between them shifted. "Let's not summon the troops just yet."

Before he could respond, she closed the space between them and kissed him. It started soft, tentative, but deepened quickly, her lips molding to his with growing confidence. Her fingers splayed across his chest, pressing against the steady beat of his heart. He reached for her waist, pulling her closer.

The night air wrapped around them, warm and humming with crickets and jasmine. When they finally pulled apart, breathless and smiling like fools, her voice was low.

"Let's just enjoy this moment for now."

Noah tucked her close, her head finding the curve of his shoulder as they swayed in rhythm with the swing. He definitely agreed. The troops could wait until tomorrow.

• • • •

EMILY LAID ALL OF GRAMS' cookbooks out on the kitchen table. The scent of coffee brewing filled the air. They'd need fuel today if they were going to plan for the cook-off.

"What am I doing?" she asked Oscar, who looked unimpressed from his spot by the fridge. "This is crazy. This cook off is in less than two weeks."

But Noah was right. If nothing else, the networking and experience would be worth it. A way to get her feet wet before diving in all the way.

A knock at the door startled her. She peeked through the curtain and smiled when she spotted Noah.

"Good morning," he said as she opened the door. He leaned in and kissed her, slow and sweet.

"Morning." She stepped aside and let him in.

"Wow," he said, eyeing the sea of cookbooks and sticky notes across the kitchen table. "Looks like you've already opened the war room."

Emily laughed. "It's either strategy... or chaos. I'm not sure which."

He chuckled. "With this crew, it could go either way."

The coffee pot had barely stopped sputtering when the rest of the troops filed in. Carly and Joey arrived with boudin and kolaches in hand.

They munched and made small talk before settling around the table. Emily smiled when Noah took the seat beside her and let his leg rest lightly against hers.

"Okay. First decision, what kind of seafood? Shrimp, crab, oysters?" She asked.

"Shrimp cooks fast," Joey said. "So does crab meat, technically."

"Good point," Emily nodded.

"What about oysters?" Noah added. "Jack Thibodeaux just launched that oyster farm. Would be great to spotlight local."

Emily nodded. "Yes, but we've got shrimp boats, too."

"Why not both? Best of Bon Chance, right?" Carly chimed in.

"I like it," Emily said. "Okay, let's see what we can find."

"Mirlitons?" Emily suggested after thumbing through a few recipes.

Joey shook his head. "Classic, but will you have time to boil them first?"

"Good point."

"What about étouffée?" Carly asked. "It's rich. Comforting. And everyone loves it."

"True," Emily said, jotting a note. "We could do a shrimp étouffée over creamy cheese grits."

Noah leaned in, pointing to a dog-eared recipe page. "What about this? Oyster Rockefeller. Maybe you could twist it somehow?"

Emily thought for a moment. "Maybe make a pasta? Add in some fried oysters or shrimp or both? I like it."

"Okay, how about a corn and crab bisque?" Joey asked. "With some kind of bread side?"

"Sounds doable." Emily mused. "But how am I going to do this all by myself?"

"Usually you can have an assistant." Joey said. "If so, I'll do it. If you want me to. I think it would be fun."

"I would love that." Having Joey as an assistant would definitely be beneficial. He was focused and competitive.

"Looks like we're going to New Orleans," Carly said, raising her coffee mug in a toast.

"We? Who's we?" Noah teased.

Carly rolled her eyes. "Like you would leave me behind."

Emily laughed, shaking her head as she reached for another sticky note. "Alright, y'all. Let's get to work. We've got one week to turn this chaos into something edible."

# Chapter Twenty

Emily curled up on the porch swing, staring out at the rain. The rain had chilled the air, and she was glad for the warmth of Grams' quilt. Oscar curled up on the edges that pooled around the chair. She could smell the gumbo simmering on the stove.

They were leaving for New Orleans the next day and her nerves were shot. The tasting had gone well. They had decided on the Oysters Rockefeller dish. Carly had even made her a playlist with "You're the Best" from Karate Kid and a song from Rocky.

Despite all the preparation, the rain and her nerves led her to the kitchen. She was more calm when her hands were busy. Grams had always said that idle hands were the devil's playthings.

She thought of Noah. He'd been so supportive this week. Hell, since she'd returned. She picked up the phone.

**Emily**: Wyd?

It wasn't long before she received a reply.

**Noah:** Just finished a run. Watching the rain.

**Emily:** Sounds cozy.

**Noah:** Want to join?

**Emily:** I have gumbo. Want some?

**Noah:** U really have to ask?

She gathered up Oscar and the blanket and went into the house. She filled a covered bowl full of the warm gumbo and put it, some cooked rice, and a loaf of crusty French bread in a bag. After patting Oscar on the head, she left for Noah's.

Her breath caught when he opened the door. He was shirtless. Her fingers itched to reach out and trace the tattoo on his chest.

"Hey," was all the conversation she could manage.

"Hey," he replied. "Come on in."

"Hungry?" she asked, lifting the bag.

His eyes darkened as he looked into her eyes. "Starving."

Her stomach fluttered.

"I'm going to shower first. Make yourself at home."

Her stomach flip-flopped.

Emily tore her eyes from his and carried the bag of food into the kitchen. She put the gumbo in a pot to warm. When she was satisfied that everything was cooking, she walked to the sliding glass doors and went out onto the deck. Sadie watched her come and go from the comfort of her doggie bed.

She leaned against the railing and watched the rain dance on the water, little droplets splattering and bouncing on the waves. The boat itself was rocking more than usual, a comforting motion that made Emily sleepy. Her own lack of sleep lately probably contributed to that. Maybe after the cook-off, she would finally get into a routine.

Emily heard Noah pad across the boat, saw his reflection in the glass as he walked up to her. He stopped behind her and wrapped his arms around her waist; he rested his chin on the top of her head. He tugged on her waist.

"Come see," he said, leading her back into the cabin of the boat and to the sofa. He left the screen door open so they could hear the rain tap lightly on the tin roof of the boat. He grabbed a blanket and patted the empty spot. She snuggled in next to him. His arm wrapped around her firmly, her head rested on his shoulder.

He was quiet, and Emily sensed he was not in the mood for mindless chatter or small talk. So, unsure of what to say, she remained quiet as well. She listened to the rain and to the steady sound of Noah's breathing. Before long, she realized he'd fallen asleep.

She slowly extricated herself from his arms to go turn off the gumbo. When she came back to the living room, he was sleeping soundly. Afraid she would wake him up if she rejoined him on the sofa, and knowing she would if she opened the door, she curled up on the small chair next to it. She wrapped a small blanket around her and put a small pillow behind her. Being here with Noah calmed her nerves and gave her a sense of peace. Maybe a nap wouldn't be so bad after all.

• • • •

EMILY AWOKE TO AN UNFAMILIAR noise. She sat up and rubbed her eyes. She listened for the sound again. It was a grunt or a moan. It was the sound of distress, and it was coming from Noah. Even in the dim light, she could see the sheen of sweat that had broken out along his body. She approached the couch slowly, unsure of what to do.

He tossed again, and the same sound came out. His breathing was short and labored. She kept a safe distance, but reached out.

"Noah," she said softly, lightly touching his shoulder. He jumped and grabbed Emily's hand. Emily tried to jerk away, but his grip was firm. His eyes were slightly unfocused, as if still caught up in whatever nightmare. He looked down, realizing he still held hers.

"Emily?"

"Yeah, I think you were having a nightmare."

His eyes were dark. He let out a sigh and released her hand. "Sorry about that."

"It's okay. Must've been a bad one."

He gave a shaky smile. "I guess you could say that."

She sat down beside him and reached for his hand. "You have them often?"

"Often enough."

"That sucks."

"Yes, it does."

"You still hungry?" Emily asked.

"Yes, I am."

"I'll get that gumbo ready," she said.

Emily busied herself warming the gumbo and making rice. It was still raining so eating on the deck was not an option. When it was all done, she carried the bowls into the living room, and Noah patted the spot next to him.

"Have a seat," he said as she handed him a bowl. He took the bowl and set it on the coffee table. "I'm going to make us a couple of drinks."

"Sounds good," she said.

He sat two drinks down and joined her on the sofa.

"Grams always said that gumbo was good for the soul," Emily said.

"She was right," Noah said, giving her a half-smile. He dipped his French bread in the gumbo and took a bite.

"Damn, Emily. You can cook."

She smiled; it was always the ultimate compliment. When she looked up from her own bowl, she noticed a small brown gumbo spot by his lip. She reached up to wipe it off, and he grabbed her hand as she touched his face. His hand covered hers as he held it in place. He pulled her fingers over to his lips and began kissing each fingertip.

Emily's stomach contracted as she stared into his eyes.

"Come here," he said softly, his voice a low invitation. He took both their bowls and put them on the coffee table. He stood and tugged her hand, leading her to the bedroom.

She didn't hesitate.

The rest of the world faded with the sound of the rain.

· · · ·

LATER, WRAPPED IN WARMTH and tangled sheets, Noah whispered, "You are amazing, Emily Thibodeaux," He gathered her close to him, spooning her.

"I didn't do much," Emily protested.

"It's just you, Emily. It's what you do to me," Noah said. He threaded his fingers with hers and raised her hands to his lips. "It's what you do for me. You are my God given solace."

Emily smiled, then started to reply. Noah put his finger to her lips., "Just enjoy, Emily. Just enjoy."

And with that, he kissed her senseless again.

# Chapter Twenty-One

E mily placed Grams' worn cookbook on the top of the clothes in the suitcase and carefully zipped it up. She didn't need it. She had memorized the recipe and practiced it many times. But bringing the cookbook was like having Grams with her.

"You ready?" Noah asked, coming up behind her. He wrapped his arms around her waist and kissed the top of her head. She tipped her head back to rest on his chest.

"As ready as I'll ever be."

So many things were racing through her head. The contest, her future. Her future with Noah. She sighed.

Noah gently turned her around. "Emily. Focus. You're going to be fine."

"I hope so."

"You will. No matter what. C'mon, let's go." He kissed her forehead and grabbed the suitcases. Emily stopped to trail a hand along her mother's quilt for luck, then followed Noah to the truck.

Noah chatted away during the short drive to New Orleans. He kept the conversation light and relaxed, and before Emily knew it, they were pulling into the hotel where she, Noah, Carly, and Joey had all booked rooms.

Carly had talked them into booking rooms at the Chateau Rouge. It had a reputation as a former bordello that was reportedly haunted by former workers and clients. The stories on the internet fascinated Carly. Joey had even talked her out of buying a ghost hunting kit she had found online. But, she had downloaded an app anyway.

Emily glanced around. She had no idea what a former bordello should look like, but if it had looked like this; it would have been a classy one.

Understated elegance was the best way to describe the lobby. Beige and blues dominated the color scheme. Fresh flowers, white lilies mostly, popped out of silver vases on the front desk, the entry tables, and even on the small end tables by the boxy sofas in the entry. Off white statues of Greek gods rested on pedestals in corners. A massive glass and brass chandelier hung down from a painted mural on the ceiling.

Emily smiled as she noticed the scantily clad figures wrapped in green vines and twisted in semi-compromising positions.

The cool blonde behind the counter saw her smile. "That's one accent we kept over the years. Why erase all the history?"

Emily shrugged, "Why, indeed?"

Noah finished checking in. "You ready to put this stuff up?"

"Sure."

Noah grabbed the bags and led the way to the room. When he opened the door, Emily's eyes lit up. The room was beautiful. Ruby red velvet covered a massive four-poster bed made of dark wood. Large red flowers bloomed from cream-colored wallpaper.

Emily crossed the room to the French doors draped in red velvet. A small wrought-iron balcony overlooked the courtyard and pool area. Tropical plants with white blooms were in clay pots on the balcony and littered around the courtyard.

"It's beautiful, Noah."

"I'm glad you like it," he said.

She turned and saw a bouquet of gardenias on the dresser. She walked over and took a deep breath, inhaling their sweet fragrance.

"These are from you?" Emily asked.

"Yes, they are. It's your weekend, Em. I'm going to pamper you."

Emily smiled and hugged him.

"Thank you, Noah."

"You're very welcome," he said, lifting her chin with a finger and kissing her gently.

"Why don't you freshen up a bit and we'll go down to the bar for a drink?"

Emily smiled. "That sounds great."

Emily plucked a bloom from the bouquet and held it to her nose.

"How would you feel about starting that pampering now, Noah?" she asked, smiling.

He smiled back. "Oh, I think I could do that."

He took the flower from her hand and tucked it behind her ear. He gathered her into his arms and kissed her.

"Happy hour can wait," he said, smiling.

"It depends on your definition of happy hour, doesn't it?" she said as Noah led her to the bed.

• • • •

WITH SHAKING HANDS, Emily shrugged on the apron that the sponsors had provided for the contestants. Luckily,

Joey was there to help. She had no idea how she was going to cut up ingredients if she couldn't calm down.

Noah was there to give her some last-minute encouragement. He grabbed her hands and brushed his lips across them after tying the apron. "You're going to be fine," he reassured her. "You know what you're doing. You've got this. Everyone who tried your recipe said it was incredible."

"Thank you."

"You're welcome."

"I have to go over to the spectator section. Take a deep breath. Focus. And wow them like you know you can," he said.

Emily smiled. How amazing he had been. So supportive. She stopped for a moment to reflect on how different her life was now. Yes, she could do this. If she could walk away from that life that had held her down for so long, she knew she could do this.

The host was a popular chef from the Food Network. She listened as he read over the rules one more time. She surveyed the cooks that were the competition. All regular people just like her. People that just loved to cook.

*I can do this.*

Her heart skipped a little beat when the host introduced the judges. Local celebrities Emeril Lagasse and John Folse were part of the judging panel. These excellent cooks would be eating her food soon, JUDGING her food.

She took another deep breath.

*I can do this.*

The host finally finished the introductions and the rules.

"Contestants, you have one hour to complete your meal," he said. "And your time begins now."

All of Emily's nervousness vanished as she began to work. She had chosen the Oysters Rockefeller pasta recipe with a shrimp crostini. Joey shucked the oysters while she prepped the rest. All the while keeping an eye on the big red time clock.

Time slipped away quickly, and before Emily knew it, the judge was giving them the ten-minute warning. It was going to be tight, but she knew she could do it. She and Joey had practiced at home with Noah and Carly being timekeepers.

Five minutes later, she began plating. Emily wanted the food to look as good as it tasted. She knew you ate with your eyes first, and she wanted everything to be flawless. She had to win this competition. Everything she dreamed about was almost a heartbeat away.

Emily finished plating as the host counted out the last ten seconds.

"Five, four, three, two, one!"

After high fiving Joey, Emily blew out a breath and looked to the spectator section. Glowing, she looked at the people that had become such good friends. They were clapping like crazy people. Emily gave them a little wave. She smiled when Noah winked.

Workers for the contest gathered up their plates for the judges.

Emily stood at her station while each judge sampled from the plates and made notations on score sheets. She felt like her heart was going to thump right out of her chest.

Finally, the judges bowed their heads together, microphones off, and compared their sheets.

"Chefs, the judges have made their decisions," the host said, taking the microphone again. "We'll start with honorable mention. Honorable Mention goes to Steve Morgan from Shreveport, Louisiana."

The host waited for the applause to die down. "Third place goes to Nathan Dupuis from Lafayette, Louisiana."

"Second place goes to Connie Melancon from Houma, Louisiana."

More applause and Emily's heart stopped beating. Who had won first?

"And now, ladies and gentlemen. The moment you have all been waiting for. This year's winner of the Southwestern Louisiana Seafood Alliance's Annual Seafood Cook-Off and winner of $25,000 is...."

Emily tried not to curse aloud as the host played up the suspense. She knew the event was being televised, but right then, the only thing she wanted was to hear who had won. Was it her? Had she won or walked away with nothing?

"Emily Thibodeaux!"

Suddenly, the breath she had been holding came out in a rush. Her eyes widened, and she swore her heart stopped beating.

The host was over at her station. "So, Ms. Thibodeaux, how do you feel right now?"

Stunned, she said, "Emeril liked my food!"

"Well, yes, apparently he did," the host said, laughing.

Noah's arms were encircling her, followed by Carly's and Joey's. She could barely breathe.

"You won, baby," Noah said, kissing her.

The host had one more question, "What do you plan to do with your money?"

"Start my catering company," she said. "The Bon Chance Catering Company."

Emily freed herself from Noah, and the rest, then went to thank the judges. She stammered when she met Emeril, like some food groupie. He smiled at her and told her to come visit his restaurant while in town. She grinned like a schoolgirl.

Finally, she rejoined the group after signing contracts and taking pictures with a blown-up $25,000 check.

"So, drinks on you tonight?" Carly asked.

"You bet. Let's get started. We have some celebrating to do."

# Epilogue

"**M**s. Thibodeaux," the man said, holding out a hand to shake, "We would be glad to use your catering company for our next company banquet. Your food is incredible."

"Thank you, Mr. Savoie. It will be a pleasure doing business with you. We'll be in touch."

"Yes, we will."

One more handshake, and Emily began clearing out the trays of samples she had brought for the presentation to the Lafayette oil company. It was the third presentation she had made that day. And the second firm confirmation.

Smiling, she loaded the van. Again, she stopped to admire the graceful green lettering, before sliding the side door closed. The same lettering adorned the wooden sign Noah had surprised her with after she had won the cook-off.

"Bon Chance Catering Company"

With a satisfied sigh, she climbed into the driver's side. Before she pulled out of the parking lot, she called Noah.

"That's two confirmations today!" she told him excitedly. "If this keeps up, I may have to hire help to keep up."

"That's great baby. Get home so we can celebrate."

"I'm on my way," she said, hanging up the phone.

She slowed to a stop as the light in front of her turned red. Emily looked up.

"Run away to the Gulf Coast," the billboard said. Emily realized she was sitting at the same red light staring at the same billboard she had stared at a year ago.

A single tear rolled down her cheek as the light turned green.

*What a difference a year could make.*

• • • •

EMILY RAN HER HANDS along Noah's arm. He was still sleeping, his face relaxed and boyish in sleep. The lines around his eyes and mouth faded. She didn't want to wake him, but couldn't resist touching him. His mouth curved in a smile, but his eyes remained shut. He reached out the same arm she'd touched and snuggled her close to him.

He had been waiting for her on the porch swing of their home. They had finished restoring Grams' home and Noah and Sadie had moved in.

Now, she nestled her cheek against his chest. He kissed the top of her head, "So tell me, Ms. Emily. What do you plan to do now that your catering company is on the verge of success? How about we celebrate with a drink at Snapper's?" Noah suggested.

"I could do that," Emily replied.

Emily smiled as they entered the bar together. She made her rounds, hugging each of the regulars. They asked how her trip to Lafayette went, and they congratulated her on her success. Finally, they took seats by Daniel.

Noah rested a hand on her thigh as Carly served them drinks. Joey poked a head out of the kitchen. "Carly? What did you do with my knife?"

She grinned, "Hang on, I'll get it."

Emily threw back her head and laughed, capturing the attention of the customers. She grinned at Noah, thinking of how much had changed since she'd returned. She'd been almost broke, homeless, friendless, and so lonely. Now, she had her own business, good friends, an actual love life, and hope for the future. Emily smiled again as Ryder joined them. He was in for the weekend and apparently ready to have a good time.

Ryder grinned and shoved his cowboy hat on Emily's head. He had given up asking her to get naked or to throw potato salad.

"Oh great," Carly said as a customer walked in. It was Cheech again. Emily rolled her eyes.

"Hey, Ms. Emily," Cheech said.

"Hi. How have you been?"

"I've been good," he laughed. "Reaaallly good."

"I bet."

"It's good to see you again. Wanna hear some music?" he asked her.

"Sure."

"What do you want to hear?"

"Anything is fine."

"Cool, man. I mean wo-man. I'm gonna play some music then."

"Great," Emily said.

Emily smiled; relieved when southern rock started drifting through the formerly quiet bar. At least he hadn't played anything too off the wall.

The door opened and Grace walked in. Her face pale.

Carly came out of the back. "Grace? Joey didn't tell me you were coming."

"I just got here this morning."

"Joey!" Carly called. "Grace just walked in." Joey's head popped through the swinging kitchen doors. "Hey Grace! You hungry?"

"Starving. Burger, please. And a beer... and maybe a shot of Patrón. It's been a hell of a day."

"Coming right up," Carly said with a grin.

"I'll Be Home for Christmas" drifted from the speakers.

Emily reached for Noah's hand, her fingers brushing his thigh. "Wanna dance?"

He stood without hesitation, threading their fingers together. "With you? Hell yes. Today, tomorrow, and every damn day. Always."

# Running on Empty

G race Delchamp stood center stage. Head lowered, she stared at the yellow wires taped to the stage through a black veil of hair. The spotlight focused on her, the heat from the light only magnified the sultry air wafting in from the open doors of the Bourbon Street bar.

Brent Mouton, the band's lead guitarist, and other singer, played the first few bars of their signature song. Grace lifted her head and began to sing. The first part of the song was acoustical. Her vocals that some had called "haunting" rang through the crowded French Quarter club accompanied only by the sound of Brent's guitar.

Her voice rose with the chorus. As she sang, the crowd melted away, along with any residual nervousness. It was simply her and the melody. Nothing else.

Grace lived for this moment. When it was her and the music. The crowd didn't matter. The applause didn't matter. For her, this was it. She thrived on it, ate it up and gave it everything she had.

Her voice trailed off as the song ended. She grinned and nodded as the crowd applauded. The next song on the set-list was a fast one, a hard rocking song from the 80s. Grace threw her hair back and played with the audience, making eye contact with the obviously single guys and winking, getting the girls in the bachelorette parties to sing along on the mic.

When everyone joined in, Grace knew then that they were all having a good time.

Song after song, the show continued, until Grace was slick with sweat and euphoria. Adrenaline coursed through her, firing her up even more.

She and Brent belted out the last few bars of the Def Leppard hit, "Pour Some Sugar on Me", and then it was break time. With a white towel in hand, she walked off the stage to the bar. She needed something cold to drink.

She held the towel to her neck with one hand while she sipped the drink with the other. Feeling a presence lurking behind her, she turned, one eyebrow raised, ready to let a drunk tourist have it.

Seeing her older brother and his best friend's smiling faces behind her, she shouted, "Joey! Carly!"

"You surprised?" Joey asked. His dark hair was, as it always was, slightly disheveled. Usually in t-shirts with off-the-wall sayings, tonight he had worn a Saints monogrammed pullover and khaki shorts.

"Yes!"

"Carly won ghost tour tickets in a writing contest, so we all came up."

I'm so excited!" Carly said. "And we're staying at the Chateau Rouge again! I hope I see a ghost this time!"

Carly had also dressed up for the night out. Her blonde hair, usually in a ponytail, floated around her shoulders. She wore a cute flowered sundress. She was often compared to Drew Barrymore, and tonight Grace could see the resemblance.

"Come on," Joey said, tucking his hand under her elbow. "Em and Noah are here. Come meet us!"

Grace followed Joey and Carly to the courtyard area, away from the crowd. Noah, an Iraq war veteran, still had issues that would probably never go away. Dealing with crowds was one. That he was in New Orleans on Bourbon Street on a weekend was a testament to how much he had changed since he and Emily had been together. Emily's quiet and calm presence probably had a lot to do with those changes. Emily had recently followed her dream and opened the Bon Chance Catering Company. She was now traveling all over southern Louisiana setting up jobs. Noah had chosen to work with his hands in solitude. He ran his own construction company. In Grace's opinion, the two could not be more perfect for each other.

Years ago, Carly, the imaginative one, had christened the group "The Boonies" one summer. "The Boonies" were loosely based on an 80s movie that had sent them all on a search for Jean Lafitte's treasure. That, and in their teens, they had considered the small coastal town of Bon Chance to be in the boondocks. It was far removed from all the action in the big cities of New Orleans, Baton Rouge, or Biloxi.

Emily and Noah were the oldest of the group. Carly and Joey were next in age. Carly was Noah's younger sister, and Joey was Grace's older brother. Carly, Joey, and Noah, had gone into business together the year before opening Snapper's Bar and Grill.

The youngest and biggest group was Grace's circle. It consisted of Grace, Ryder, Gabriel, and Benjamin. Benjamin, Carly and Noah's younger brother, had passed away a few years ago in an oil rig accident.

"I see your friends are here," Brent said, walking up behind Grace. Grace stiffened and resisted the urge to roll her eyes.

Things with her and Brent had become tense lately. He kept asking her out for dinner, for drinks, for sex, which Grace kept refusing. The man was much too self-absorbed and arrogant for her taste. Grace could see the train wreck that getting involved with him would be from a mile away. Brent had grown up in Pointe Shade, a small town just down the road from Bon Chance. He was a Mouton, and that meant trouble. His uncle thought he owned the town and probably did own most of it. As a result, his kinfolk thought that everything else belonged to them. Even women.

"Yes, Brent."

"We're here for a ghost tour and Bourbon Street, of course." Carly chimed, always ready for a party. Brent's eyes shifted to the blond beauty.

*Oh Lord*, Grace thought, *here we go.*

"Well, hello Carly. You look amazing tonight, as usual."

Grace cut her eyes to Joey, who was frowning. As was Noah. But Carly could handle herself.

"And don't you look....sweaty," Carly said, smiling with a wrinkle of her nose. It was a jab, and Grace resisted the urge to laugh.

Brent frowned, his blue eyes narrowed. He turned to Grace. "Well, we're back up in five minutes."

"I'll be there."

Brent disappeared back through the crowd in the bar.

"What was that all about?" Carly asked as soon as he was gone.

"Oh, he's being an ass. He gets more conceited every day. He thinks he's God's gift to women. And doesn't like taking no for an answer. No matter how many times you turn him down. It's getting aggravating."

Carly shook her head, "Men!"

"It's nothing I can't handle," Grace said, downing her drink as she looked at her phone. "Well, guys, it's time for me to get back up there. I'll see y'all soon." She said, hugging them. "Have fun!"

. . . .

**FREE on Kindle Unlimted**

**Click here to buy —>https://amzn.to/3I0Er0W**

**Click here to download a sample —->https://dl.bookfunnel.com/zumqp1klgv**

# Don't miss out!

Visit the website below and you can sign up to receive emails whenever A. L. Vincent publishes a new book. There's no charge and no obligation.

https://books2read.com/r/B-A-FJAK-BBHLB

**BOOKS 2 READ**

Connecting independent readers to independent writers.

# Also by A. L. Vincent

**Bon Chance Boonies**
Tangled up In You